Sick Burn Cut

Sick Burn Cut

(*At Last, the Appearance of Our Lady of the Ugly Ones, in Spokane*)

Deran Ludd

Semiotext(e) Native Agents Series

This book is dedicated to my mentor, the late great
Steven Jesse Bernstein.
Jesse was Seattle's premiere writer and he was one of the first
people who really believed in me as a writer and for that
and for his years of friendship and for all the long late-night talks
on the phone I will always love him. I'll see you there Jesse...

Thanks to my 3rd grade remedial reading teacher. Special thanks to
Katherine Francillon and Chris Kraus. Thanks to Christine Strati,
Jennifer Thompson, Dick Kallich, Paul Hoskin, Brad, Ruby X, Wade,
Carlo, Sharon, Sue Ann, Timothy, John, Dominick, Alice.

Any resemblance between characters in this story and real living
human beings is strictly a randomized coincidence.

Portions of this text appear in a somewhat different form in the
book *New York Writing* published by Merve Verlag, Berlin.
Other writings by Deran Ludd have appeared in the magazines
Patio Table, Hopeless Tasks, Discipline, Zero Hour and the
Semiotext(e) USA issue.

Back cover photo: Bob Berg

Semiotext(e)
522 Philosophy Hall
Columbia University
New York, New York 10027

(718) 387-6471

Printed in the United States of America.

Sick Burn Cut

1

"In the name of God, the Compassionate, the Merciful.

...And commemorated in the Book is the story of Mary.
How she left her people for a solitary place in the East
and there remained alone with her cloak.
How We sent unto her an angel of Ours
in the shape of a grown man,
a Companion without fault.
And when she saw him she called out:
'May the Merciful defend me from you!
If you fear God leave me and go your way!'
The Companion said:
'I am a messenger from the Divine,
to give unto you a boy most pure'..."

> *The Quran*
> Sura 19, "Mariam" (Mary)

2

SEATTLE

"This is the hand... the hand grips... the grip is not too clean... or careful..."

Bound as he is to the four corners of a large square wooden frame, and with the frame tilted so his head is very near the gray linoleum floor, Mary cannot clearly see the hand. Even craning his neck and head up as far as they will go he cannot really see the hand. The focus of the rows of pinlights is too tight, lighting only the immediate area of the frame, leaving the rest of the room in more or less darkness. But, with his head twisted up and to one side Mary can see the tool the hand is holding, gleaming and black, that has been shoved into the glare. Trying to get a good look at it, Mary squints and fights against the injection he has just been given. But the tool disappears back into the darkness and Mary lets his head drop back onto the weave of leather strips.

In the darkness just beyond the frame an indeterminate number of men watch and wait for the shot to take hold so that they can play some more.

Through the floor and the frame Mary can feel the dull persistent thud of House music rumbling from the main room of Mr. Clark's party.

Very soon Mary is glowing inside. Warmth spreads throughout his body and his mind floats relaxed and nearly unconscious.

The playroom's attendant, dressed in his crisp white nurse's outfit, approaches Mary, cool and reserved like a mortician called in on his day off. He checks the pulse, then draws up the eyelids and flashes a small light at Mary's pupils to ascertain constriction. He puts his stethoscope on Mary's back and listens a moment. He grabs a handful of Mary's left buttock and squeezes, hard. Satisfied his duty is done, the attendant steps back into the darkness and in a quiet rasp says:

"Alright gentlemen, you may begin again."

The frame is now tilted so that Mary is horizontal. A dozen hands commence a thorough and exacting exploration of his body. Latex-gloved fingers in his mouth and rectum.

Mary shifts back into a vague consciousness and listens in on considerations as to where the metal clamps should be applied. The men's voices are cool and quiet, with just an edge of testosterone. Their contemplations are interrupted by the attendant's rasping admonishments.

"No, no, no! Gentlemen, please. The skin will begin to tear if that clamp is tightened further..."

There is a certain amount of frustrated muttering from among the guests.

3

On one side blasts of wind and rain off Puget Sound shake the two 10th-floor hotel room windows in their old wooden frames. On the other side Ruby has a hand up, palm pressed to the glass of one of these windows (if you are inside the room facing the windows, this window is on the left). In her other hand a dozen or so playing cards arranged by suit. A scowl is on her face. Her eyes flipping from her cards to 2nd Avenue 10 floors down. Past the Savoy Hotel's neon sign that runs from floors 8 to 6 down to the street.

Ruby's eyes hold on three people who've just gotten off

a southbound bus across the street from the Savoy. None of the three figures cross 2nd toward the hotel. The rumble of its diesel engine is very distant and muffled as the bus pulls away from the curb.

Edith looks from the back of Ruby's close-fitting red cocktail dress to across the table at his Canasta partner Jane. Jane's face says nothing. She pushes her half-frame reading glasses up the bridge of her nose and continues studying her own cards, the card face up on the top of the discard pile and the cards melded on the table in front of Murrow.

Murrow is also watching Ruby's back. Murrow's lips twitch in a familiar and involuntary sneer. She sets down her cards, picks up the blue plastic pouch of Drum tobacco and rolls a slender cigarette. As she lights it she sees Edith is back staring at Ruby, his plucked and blackened eyebrows drawn together in anxiety. Murrow's lips twitch again and she ignores them all, watching the smoke puff and swirl from her mouth.

Her strategy for the rest of this hand firm in her mind Jane finally looks up at the other two people at the table. She sees Ruby's chair is empty but she does not turn to look for Ruby. Instead Jane looks toward the windows but over at her husband John. John is not playing Canasta. He is wrapped up in the TV which faces the window on the right. He lifts his glass and sips at his Martini. He sees Jane's look, then sees the game has stopped, and snatches a glance in Ruby's direction. He looks back at Jane, then Murrow and Edith, then Ruby, then Jane again and shrugs. He returns his focus to the TV.

Jane looks up to where the wall opposite her and the ceiling meet. She can see Murrow's puffs of smoke roll into her line of vision but she does not look at Murrow (who is sitting to her right). Jane sighs, sets down her cards and leans back in her chair until it is balanced on the two back legs and braced in place by her right foot on the linoleum. She pushes her hair from her face, tucks it behind her ears, plucks off her reading glasses and lets them dangle from the cord around her neck. Looking from Edith to Murrow Jane purses her lips and exhales loudly through her nose. Murrow is staring at the table top and smoking. Edith and Jane exchange looks. Finally Jane turns her head a little to the left. Not so that she can really see Ruby, but so that her voice is projected in that general direction.

"He's *not* gonna come here when he's done. I mean, I doubt it, don't you? Would you? He'll go home afterwards. Wash and then sleep I expect. Don't you think?

"Besides, you're the boss *Ruby*. You said it was up to him if he wanted to work there again. Didn'tcha? And anyway, it's just 1am. He won't be done for hours."

Her tone lowers and softens just slightly.

"Not only is it your turn, but your Martini is getting warm. I'll drink it if you're gonna waste it..."

Murrow jabs her cigarette over the ashtray and taps it violently, the ash misses and hits the table and Murrow brushes it onto the floor. She scowls and looks around the room at its occupants. Her gaze stops on Ruby.

"Mary's a shit for goin' ahead and doin' it again! Like he doesn't have enough to keep his ass busy! Dumbfuck!"

Murrow puffs furiously at her cigarette. Ruby suddenly

turns toward the table.

"Alright! *All-fucking-right!* I'll play. I wasn't saying nothing about Mary. Was I? No. And don't touch my drink!"

Ruby stalks back and drops with a thud into her chair (which puts her back to the windows).

Even sitting you can see Ruby is taller than any of them. Almost as tall as Mary. She drops her cards to the table face down, grabs her glass and gulps down the rest of her Martini. Before picking the cards back up she pokes and prods the vast, twisted and ratted mass of her black hair. She shifts around in her chair, takes up her hand, draws a card, adds two jacks to a meld she and Murrow have going, then flings a four onto the discard pile and returns her hand to the table facedown.

It's Edith's turn now (he is to Ruby's left). He is very relieved to be playing again and smiles as he takes the upcard off the stock and tries to figure out what to play. Murrow's rolling another cigarette. She keeps staring at Edith and Ruby because they are the closest to Mary of anyone in the posse. To her this means they should have stopped him from working Clark's Christmas party again. Edith is busy trying to remember who has picked up and discarded what and so doesn't see Murrow's glares. Ruby sees her girlfriend's looks but pretends not to and stares at nothing as she thinks. Murrow's irritation erupts.

"He's a fuckin' shithead! He doesn't need the money. What's he trying to prove, and who's he tryin' to prove it to?... He did *one* of Clark's parties and everyone acted like that was some sorta fuckin' badge of honor or some such shit. Then he does another, and now a third!... Maybe we oughta talk to Husayn about it... maybe Mary just likes it, huh..."

She fumbles for her pack of tobacco.

"And why the fuck didn't Husayn do something?! Shit, Husayn just packs and goes to Portland! Shit. They're both assholes. We can take care of them, they don't need the goddamn money..."

Cigarette rolled she pauses to light it, exhales and waves her left hand in front of her.

"What if he wants to do *another*?! *Then* are you gonna say somethin' Ruby?!"

"Alright Murrow. Enough."

"Hey! I got some say in posse business too! And I tellya he's *not* gonna do anything *this* stupid again.

"If it had been some other Straight Shooter you woulda stomped on their fuckin' head!"

"Shut-the-fuck-up!"

Nobody talks while Edith finishes playing. Now it's Murrow's turn. She uses this focus to resume her tirade with a snarl.

"If we have to go and find'm, or he gets all fucked up... I'm gonna give that boy some shit! I don't give a fuck if he is your lieutenant!"

She looks pointedly at Ruby as she says this last bit. Without looking away from the TV screen John interjects:

"When he gets home, if he wants to and he's up to it, he'll call. He knows where we all live..."

Murrow fumes but goes ahead with her play.

It's back around to Jane now. Jane's glasses are back up on her nose and she scans her memory for who's played what. She stares at the back of Ruby's cards trying to calculate what she has. Murrow's not bad at Canasta, but Ruby is the real challenge. Edith sets down his hand and stretches, leaning back in his chair. He has been daydreaming about a man he'd danced with last night. He yawns and says:

"On my way home I'm gonna go by the Strand and see if he's back and in one piece. Then I can call whoever wants me to."

Clutching the stem, Ruby is tapping the base of her Martini glass on the table, still thinking and trying to ignore the chatter. She looks down at her empty glass, she stands up. On this cue Edith also rises, empty cocktail glass in hand.

"More Martinis?"

For a minute there is no response. All eyes are on Jane and the natural canasta she is laying down. Nothing is said as she continues laying down all her cards and goes out. Edith snaps his fingers and laughs.

"I love being her partner. It's almost as good as having a boyfriend..."

Murrow reaches across the table, picks up Jane's empty glass and hands it and her own to Edith. Edith turns to John.

"John?"

"Mmm... no thanks, I'm fine."

Ruby yawns and says:

"I'll assist."

At the cracked formica countertop of the room's small kitchenette Ruby rinses the shaker out, fills it with ice and splashes in a small touch of vermouth. Edith slices twists off a lemon. He pauses and turns toward Jane.

"How'd we do?"

By way of reply Jane starts adding out loud.

"... plus fifty is sixteen thirty, plus one twenty is seventeen fifty... plus my natural is twenty-two fifty and two hundred for going out is twenty-four fifty..."

Jane smiles slightly, Edith smiles broadly and turns back to slicing off twists. Done shaking the ice and vermouth together Ruby drains off most of the vermouth. Jane removes her reading glasses and watches the Martini production line. She squints a bit and frowns for a second.

"How long have we all known each other? Five, six years? And I still don't like my Martinis as dry as you three. Right? Huh? And yet you persist in trying to... convert me... to the Very Dry Martini."

"So?"

"So add some vermouth to my glass. And make it a double while you're at it."

"Yeah, yeah. A very *damp* double for Jane."

Ruby and Edith mix, shake, pour and garnish the cocktails in brief, simple motions. Familiarity with the terrain. When they're done Ruby steps back and points from glass to glass in review.

"Double olive, twist, twist, twist."

4

After dumping Mary on the floor (and not the bed), Mr. Clark's servants are thoughtful enough to pull down the blinds of Mary's room at the front of the 3rd floor of the Strand Hotel. Standing over him one of them empties a papersack full of cash that users of the gameroom left as tips for Mary's good services. A few of the crinkled and folded bills scatter on top of him, but most pile up next to Mary's stomach on the linoleum floor. On the formica-topped chrome-legged kitchen table (that has one end resting against the wall with the room's two windows) the servants leave a little cardboard box containing four disposable syringes loaded with hefty doses of morphine. With a fifth hypo of morphine they give Mary a hit to help him stay asleep. They swab his arm with a disposable alcohol pad where the injection has just been given. Mr. Clark is so nice, he thinks of everything.

On 1st Avenue, three floors down, the truck that delivers the weekend supply of beer to Cigarette (which is almost directly across the street from the Strand) pulls into traffic without looking. Narrowly missing a sedan with family of five inside; tourists lost in transit from the Space Needle to the Pike Place Market. The drivers of both vehicles lean on their car horns. It is this noise, hours later (nearly three in the afternoon) that jolts Mary's mind on its way back to consciousness.

Closer and closer to awake his mind starts registering all his pain. Pain all over. Not fully awake yet Mary twitches and convulses as the pains tremor through his nervous system, back and forth in all parts of his body. Mary groans through his nose and clenched teeth. He coughs, chokes and weakly spits a mouthful of mucous streaked with a bit of blood onto the floor. He groans again, loudly, from his now open mouth.

Mary parts his eyelids enough to recognize where he is. He tries to stretch out his legs. All he feels is pain, he can't really tell if his legs have moved or not. Mary lies still awhile longer and then slowly, slowly shifts from his right side onto his belly. He drags himself to the kitchen table which abuts the room's windows. Using one of the chairs as a prop he pulls himself up onto his knees. One arm on the chair's seat holds him upright, the other hand gropes for the small box and its syringes he knows is on the table. Clutching the box he slumps back to laying on his left side on the floor. After he catches his breath from this exertion Mary manages to find a vein and keep the needle steady enough to get a clean hit.

Once the morphine has kicked in, and the harsher edges are dulled, Mary makes his way to the bed. With both pillows under his butt he is able to semi-comfortably sit up with his back to the wall. An ashtray is found and Mary lights a filterless Lucky Strike cigarette. For a few minutes he just sits and smokes and is glad to be back in his room. His butt does not hurt as much as he remembers from the previous time. He rummages through haphazard piles of cassettes on the linoleum between the bed (a mattress on the floor) and the boombox. He settles on a C-90 compilation he's made of favorite Velvet Underground tunes.

He listens to the music and stares at the pile of cash still on the floor (which, later counted, totals eighteen hundred and twenty-two dollars). Before he nods out Mary calls Ruby and then Edith. Ruby is curt and matter-of-fact at first. Once she's sure he's okay she lightens up and they chat briefly. Edith (who is Mary's younger cousin as well as a partner) is initially cool as well. But soon his long-time admiration for his older cousin gushes out and Edith oohs and aahs in appropriate places during Mary's synopsis of the night's events. Mary describes particular bruises and welts on his body as punctuation for the tale. Edith does not tell Mary that he'd used his copy of Mary's room key to look in on him an hour or so after noon.

5

MARY

There *are* things I depend on to anchor me to the world. This Smith & Wesson .38-caliber revolver (the M-28 "Highway Patrolman" with a four-inch barrel and matte black plastic grip). These clothes. This face and these features. These are the things that have lasted.

There are fewer humans than dresses that I would ever depend on. Well, I mean, of course, there is Husayn. And Ruby, and Edith, and John, Jane, Murrow, Charlie, Bontemp... any of the other Straight Shooters I suppose. No. Only Husayn and Ruby. I hate trusting anyone to guard my back, but you end up having to in a pinch. I just try my best to keep out of *those* sorts of situations.

I mean, I do trust Edith. He's my cousin and I've known him forever. But, his reflexes... in a tight spot... they are not always so sure or right on the mark. He's tougher than most men, but he can lose his cool too easily. Just look at the trouble he has with scaring away boyfriends, and I'm not saying that to talk behind his back. I'm just saying, as a for instance.

So I guess besides Husayn there's really only Ruby.

Ruby. Me and her, we've been partners all the years I've lived in Seattle. She was my first friend in Seattle after I left mom's in Portland, Oregon. And what was that? 14 years ago?

I've got a huge amount of respect for her; she's sharp. No one fucks with Ruby's leadership... except maybe her girlfriend Murrow... she's got the power and uses it.

One thing though... I've never understood her fetish for those little Ingram M-11s. Yeah, yeah, they took her through her youth and all. But. The more automated a firearm the more unreliable. In my opinion. I don't care how many rounds a second it spits if it's gonna be jammin' all the time. Or even occasionally, it's those *occasions* when you really need the firepower. Whatever.

Otherwise there's nothing I'd ever say against her. Shit, the whole plan for us to get a posse and take over Belltown was hers. The Straight Shooters, the whole thing, all hers. Even the name. She got it from some old radio show for kids or something. I dunno exactly how she ever heard it.

Anyway, the possibility was there for years, but it was Ruby who had the plan.

We talk. All the time we talk. Nowadays Ruby talks about being too old and shit to be the Maximum Leader. Too old to be in the streets motivating and recruiting the teenagers. At first when she was saying these things I got tight and tense thinking she was trying to turn on us. But Ruby doesn't say anything in *that* tone of voice that isn't mostly true.

So, I started watching things and thinking. I start to see that it's pretty much all true... our days are fading... just a matter of time... the kids aren't joining posses like Straight Shooters so much anymore. The gangs that are growing and fighting their way up are all mixed up with religion or politics. Crime and protection are all being organized as Baptist, Marxist, Sivaist, Catholic, Anarchist or whatever... our day is fading, our promise mostly used up...

6

MARY

Back then, I guess about eight years ago, Belltown was in between rulers... the Mallrats had just driven out the Marielitos. Pushed them way south of Stewart Street. The Mallrats were these suburban kids with bigger hair than brains. No one was looking forward to when they would show up in force to claim their spoils and install their regime. On top of this the police were taking advantage of the power vacuum to do what cops do best — pressuring, intimidating and stealing.

Like I said, the Mallrats were these suburban kids, east-of-the-lake-types mostly; Bellevue, Mercer Island, Kirkland, who'd gotten bored with the malls and cul-de-sacs they already dominated. They wanted some new turf, something in the big city. New people to notice and obey them, new people to intimidate. These bugs weren't any tougher than any of those other suburban posses — all style: no strategy, no tactics, just looks and ferocity.

With no new boot on our faces quite yet we were hanging out and lounging in make-believe contentment. Crowded into the Frontier Room buying each other drinks and complaining.

One of the small tables in the middle of the lounge was cleared of glasses and chairs and people'd laid out different little piles and lines of cocaine and a bunch of very fine China White the neighborhood's main supplier, Eagle Chief, had pulled out of somewhere to celebrate the brief smell of freedom. The dope on one side and the coke on the other. People did a little of one or the other, or sniffed up a speedball. Everyone throwing in their two cents' worth on how dreadful it was gonna be when the metalheads set the marching orders.

"Who knows how much they'll up the protection..."

"Yeah but how will they affect the flow and *quality* of drugs?"

"Worse yet — what if they try and move in and take over the Frontier Room or Cigarette?"

"Those haircuts! And that music, all those bad guitar solos..."

"I'm already missing the Salsa and Merengue..."

Me and Ruby had talked it all over a couple days earlier. Neither of us believed for a second that these Mallrats could really keep their shit together and keep the cops out and other posses from raiding and pillaging or trying to take over. Belltown would probably end up shredded and unlivable from warring factions.

That particular night, the night things got moving, was like all others. By 10pm the daytime regulars (retired sailors and Social Security recipients) had all crawled home. The same fifty thirsty "failed prospects" were left to hold up the bar.

Milling back and forth, alone and in knots. Cigarette to the Frontier Room and back. Cigarette for dancing and the Frontier Room for lounging and conversation. The two places are right next door to each other, separated only by the door to the Oregon Hotel which takes up the two floors above them. All of us loud and trashy and drinking like a drought had just ended. Same small-talk, same waiting for something to happen. Same rainy night, drizzling and pouring in turn. From the Frontier Room's front door, past the cafe counter on the right, past the fake wood paneling, past the three booths across from the counter on the left that are for eating during the day and for the spillover crowd from the lounge in back at night... a trail of drips, muddy puddles and soggy cigarette butts on worn linoleum.

I was parked in the furthest back of the three booths in the small lounge area. Cracked white formica table top, ripped burnt orange vinyl seats. Listening (sort of) to the same thing over and over. Staring up at one of the illuminated beer signs on the wall... same mountain stream, same guy in hip boots casting his fishing line and tossing his empty beer can into the water...

I'd been trying to get Ruby to pull up a chair or squeeze into the seat beside me all evening. She sits down a second and then jumps up, poking her face into different knots of people sitting and standing around. Coming back over to the table with a sly smile on her lips.

She's up to something that's for sure. She keeps circulating — around and around the lounge, then out front to the cafe area. Buttonholing people as they come in the front door and pause to shake the rain off.

Next time I look up Ruby's over by the jukebox arguing with these two guys. I get up and work my way through the crowd to her side. Not that she can't handle two guys like that just fine on her own, but I've always liked trouble too. When I show up the two jerks get even tenser and then split.

"Dumbfucks..."

"Alright Ruby. What's up?"

"Honey, we're gonna do it... we're gonna take it all."

I look irritated and she smiles smug-like.

"Give me a couple more minutes to see if I got to everyone that counts, then you'll get the details."

She spots a table she thinks she hasn't hit yet and starts to head off. She stops and comes back to me. Lips to my ear she says:

"I don't have to tell you Mary, 'cause I know you're gonna go for it. It's gonna be you and me running things..."

This time when she starts to walk away the two guys she'd just been arguing with come back. The taller peroxide blond (not as tall as me, but nearly as tall as Ruby) points a finger at Ruby and yells over the music:

"I'm not going along with anyone's fucking plan if I don't

think it can work! And your ideas are just plain shit-crazy!"

In reply Ruby raises her arms and shoves him hard in the chest. He crashes back into the jukebox, sending the needle scratching across Patsy Cline. His friend starts to step in, I move between him and Ruby. He stops and glares up at me.

Ruby looks at me and then them and then the room full of people. Strands of black hair drooping across her face. She shrugs.

Ruby steps around to one side and reaches behind the jukebox. After fishing for a moment she yanks the cord and the loud music is suddenly gone. The yelling needed for conversation in the lounge, suddenly without its musical accompaniment, becomes its own blaring mish-mash. It takes nearly a minute for everyone to realize something is happening. As they start shutting up and looking in our direction Ruby jerks a chair out from under someone at a nearby table and drags it in front of the darkened jukebox. I move a little closer to spot her as she stands on it, her pumps' heels gouging holes in the chair's vinyl-covered seat.

"This *asshole*..."

She gestures at the man she'd pushed.

"... thinks we gotta be *careful*. Just wait for those bugs from the burbs to move in and set up shop. *He* says we can't ever, *ever* raise a finger in our own defense. 'Dig in and cover your head.' Sit around and whine is more like it! Put up with whoever, and their cheap threats, and bad drugs at god *knows* what sort of prices!..."

The guy she's using as a scapegoat makes feeble protes-tations of being misrepresented. But Ruby has everyone's attention. She pauses, fierce eyes piercing out through the ratted strands of hair that partially shroud her face, hands on hips, slowly scanning the crowd. Expectant faces peering at her from the dark.

"These dumbfucks from the burbs want a new *playground*... so we gotta put up with their bad haircuts and awful fucking music... pushing their groping fingers around... and they're not gonna be so indifferent to this place, or Cigarette. Any of you wanna share a booth with one of those? And I never heard of these metalhead types being too... tolerant or 'kind' about queers... know what I mean? Bugs infesting everything. *They* are gonna be *our* bosses?!

"Shit, if I bow and scrape any lower I'll be dragging my tits on the sidewalk!..."

Ruby waves her hands to quiet them again.

"*But!* Give me 10, 20, 30 of you, and one week, and I could tie this neighborhood up so tight those Mallrats couldn't even get their tiny pricks in here! It could be *ours!* All ours!

"There's enough experience and connections in this room, right now tonight, for us to run the show. Easy! Fuck it! 10 of you with your guns and I could do it by *this* weekend!

"Same storyline but with *us* in control... our show, our power... and I'd rather die fucking trying than put up with new masters!"

The crowd hoots and stomps with approval. Ruby lets this go on for a minute. I walk over to our booth and bring back my half-finished Martini. I take a sip and hand it to Ruby, she smiles and gulps the rest in one swallow. People start quieting down and talking among themselves. So as not to lose their focus Ruby lifts her hand for silence, there is quick compliance. She is already our leader.

"Now... I'm not saying someone bigger and stronger won't come along and put our faces back under the boot... but right now, we've got the best fucking chance we've ever had to strike out on our own....

"The Mallrats didn't defeat the Marielitos because they're bigger, or smarter! *Hardly.* I mean, half the Marielitos' bosses and best soldiers are still in jail from that raid on the Gatesburg Hotel a month ago. The Mallrats just happened to be in the right place at the right time. If the Mallrats do take over you can bet the Marielitos, the Southend Crew, the Fiances, whoever, will make an attempt to move in and throw out those assholes inside a month. There's no fucking way they can hold on to Belltown. No... fucking... way...."

Ruby gets down and pushes her way over to the booth where she'd left her purse. Back standing on the chair she opens and rummages in it a second and then pulls out her Ingram machinepistol. She hands me her purse and starts waving the M-11 over her head yelling. Near silence falls over the room.

"Take out your guns! Guns out! All guns out!"

Ruby keeps chanting this and everyone scrambles to unholster or take out of pockets and purses a wide variety of firearms. I realize this is good showmanship and a good playing of the crowd, but I'm hoping everyone keeps it together enough not to start pulling triggers.

"And so what if we can't have a better life? We could have a good death..."

The crowd shrieks their approval. Ruby jumps down and

people surge forward surrounding her with their own pledges of loyalty and admiration.

The bartender and the waitress are huddled back behind the bar. Lee the bartender discreetly switches the safety of the sawed-off shotgun under the bar to the off position. She trusts Ruby, but this rabble-rousing can bring out all sorts of nasty troublemakers. Her girlfriend Arlen, who's the waitress, is less cautious and climbs up on a stool and lets loose with her piercing two-finger whistle to show her support for Ruby. Now Lee likes what's being said too but she's got to keep the business open and selling drinks. Once I'm sure Ruby's done I make my way back to the bar to give Lee some words of reassurance. I pull Arlen down from the stool and climb up it myself and yell:

"The bar's still open for business."

The crowd responds with a rush of orders and firearms are put back to rest.

Ruby was right of course. About all of it. And she was right about my being into the plan without a second thought. I never liked the way most people I know just sit around and take whatever shit is dished them. A bad habit they'd developed.

All through this Edith's eyes are bugging out. He squirms around in the booth seat. He jumps up, jarring the table, drinks sloshing. His mouth working open and closed, open and closed and he almost says something several times but stops. He sits down. Edith keeps gripping the thigh of a young man he cajoled into sitting with him.

Soon the boy gets up and leaves with his upper right thigh red and bruised.

After there's been time for everyone to refresh their drinks and talk it over among themselves Ruby returns to her podium. A new Martini in hand she sips it several times before she goes back to prodding and seducing. Not nearly so frantic now. More like a co-conspirator. Answering questions and instilling confidence. The pumps of leadership fit her perfectly. 15, 20 minutes and Ruby feels certain her plan is firmly implanted in the crowd's desires. So she gets down off the chair, brushes off the seat, returns it to the woman she'd taken it from, yells for another Martini and plugs the jukebox back in.

With Edith and me in tow she circulates from table to table, farming out tasks that need to be taken care of immediately. Without the two of us discussing it Ruby starts referring to me as her lieutenant.

The Frontier Room has a payphone near the door and two in back by the bathrooms. All are kept busy. Plans laid, allegiances confirmed, businesses franchised.

Once we've got things going and the momentum is there Ruby goes back behind the bar to the office to use the phone in relative quiet. This is the call that will make or break the plan. Cool and steady she talks for 10 minutes with one of the most powerful people in Seattle. A Native American woman named Eagle Chief.

Eagle Chief is the boss of the 1st Avenue Tribe.

In downtown Seattle, control of the streets changes as posses come and go. But no matter who the players are in the street, the 1st Avenue Tribe is the director backstage. They wholesale the drugs and make available what weapons they want on the streets and only to those they want to have them. If Eagle Chief and her lieutenants don't like you, and you're the current force in a particular neighborhood, they'll do business with you. For now. But you won't last long. If they decide you're a bunch of greedy assholes they start turning screws and by the by — you're gone.

A dozen years ago the Native American population downtown was drowning in alcoholism and poverty. Eagle Chief shows up and sets up a shamanistic center in a storefront on 1st Avenue near Blanchard Street. Inside three years she has welded most of the Native Americans regardless of tribe of birth into the 1st Avenue Tribe. Over a few years they gradually expand into other neighborhoods until the 1st Avenue Tribe settles into the city's background. Pulling chains and making deals. And our downtown was a whole new deal. Ruby and Eagle Chief have been friends for a long time, probably as far back as when Eagle Chief made her first appearance in Belltown.

Half an hour after Ruby's phone call, Eagle Chief's big black sedan pulls up out front of the Frontier Room. Eagle Chief and five bodyguards and lieutenants are let in. Hugs are exchanged. Cups of coffee are ceremonially shared. Then new arrangements are all laid out. Eagle Chief cuts wholesale drug prices and Ruby agrees to move 30% more than the Marielitos were. Eagle Chief gives a little speech praising our efforts and wishing us success, everyone (even me) feels a bit more confident and excited.

After 2am Lee sends Arlen and the shortorder cook home. Lee stays around to keep an eye on the place, serve a few drinks, and watch the color TV. Periodically she throws in her opinions.

At 6am the Frontier Room's day shift and the first-thing-in-the-morning drinkers show up. At first they're all quiet and cautious, watching out of the corners of their eyes those of us still wrapping up business. Obviously rumors of the night's meeting has indeed gotten around. Once they suss out that it is all a good thing everyone loosens up and bellies to the bar they toast to our success.

We night-timers put on our coats and scuttle out into the damp gray Seattle morning.

7

Either Jane or John drove whatever car was being used. Always.

Jane liked to drive fast because she liked to think she had somewhere urgent to get to. John drove recklessly because he liked to think he had something to lose.

Tonight it is John and Jane's '72 four-door sedan. Tonight Jane is the hands on the wheel and she's pushing 60 down 2nd Avenue so that we may make all the traffic lights. Edith and Mary are stuffed into the front seat next to her. Edith is in the middle and he and Jane are busy with their current favorite routine. Cackling and hooting, caustic and loud.

Mary is quiet, face to the passenger window. Watching the city zoom by and the rain splatter the window. Mary has moved as close to the door as he can get to physically remove himself from any attempts to be included in Jane and Edith's playing. Mary would like to roll the window all the way down, crank up the cassette of The Fall that is playing on the car stereo, and just drive around in the storm. But he knows even suggesting this as an alternative to going to the speak-easy in some Pioneer Square artist's loft isn't worth all the complaints that will come up.

Mary digs a slightly crumpled Lucky Strike out of his handbag. As he lights it he watches two people huddled in a Metro bus stop shelter for the second the car shoots by. Neither of these people looks like Sayyid Husayn, but they remind him of not having his boyfriend at hand. Sayyid Husayn still has not returned after being gone for two weeks. Mary has almost completely healed from his job at Mr. Clark's. Any day now Mary expects Sayyid Husayn's key in the door of their room at the Strand. He (almost) resents Sayyid Husayn expressing his disapproval of the gig at Clark's by leaving the city for an undisclosed length of time.

They'd gone to see this showcase of local bands. And the show had been shit, a nightmare. They hadn't stayed long enough to do much asking around to see if anyone had seen Sayyid Husayn.

The whole scene was made unpleasant by the flood of frat boys and suburban waste products in their Benetton and

Gap hipwear. Murrow picked a few pockets, but didn't snatch anything worth the time spent at it. They'd wanted to stay and see the headliner, Mudhoney, but there were just too many opening acts to suffer through. Soulless pose bands trying to pass themselves off as something they'd read about in Spin or Thrasher.

"No, no. *I'm* Mavis and you're Missy!"

"No, I'm Mavis and *you're* Missy!"

"Not on your life! *I'm* Josef Stalin. And *you,* yes you, are Mavis!"

"Never!"

"*Always!*"

"No, no, no! I'm Uncle Joe, and you're the thing in polyester plaid!"

"Mavis *never* wears plaid. So, I *must* be Mavis and you Missy..."

Murrow leans over the car seat from the back and interrupts.

"You two are ruining the game with this famous dictator shit. And I think we've had enough of it for now anyway..."

Jane sneers into the rearview mirror at Murrow.

"*You* are going to Siberia!"

Edith lights a cigarette, then takes a swig from the fifth of brandy. He turns around to Murrow, John and Ruby in the back seat and hands them the fifth.

"You're right, you are *so* right! I'll settle this whole unfortunate business once and for all... *I'm* Mavis, *she's* Missy, and..."

He jerks around and pokes Mary in the arm.

"... *he's* Joey Stalin! Am I right or what?!"

Jane and Edith cackle and Murrow glowers as she passes the fifth to John.

Mary snaps his focus from outside to Edith. He glares with uncontrolled frustration and resentment. Edith drops his smile and looks regretfully at his cousin.

"I'm not fucking Missy, Mavis, Pam, or Stalin! In fact, I'm not even here!"

Edith looks pained, Jane rolls her eyes, Mary grabs the door handle, pulls it and flings the door open. Rain and wind burst in and Jane slams on the brakes as she twists the steering wheel to keep the car from spinning. She moves the car to the right and it skids to the curb. Before it is fully stopped Mary hurls himself out the door, stumbling at first, then dashing to the sidewalk. Right behind him Edith is out on the pavement, clutching his coat against the rain. Ruby has the back window rolled down. Edith is yelling:

"Mary! Mary! Please! I'm sorry! Whatever! We'll skip the speak-easy and go back to the Frontier Room. *Mary!*"

Ruby sticks her head out into the rain.

"Goddamnit Mary! Get the fuck back in the car!"

Jane is leaning forward over the wheel, watching Mary with no expression, not even curiosity, on her face. She'd figured Mary's mood out first thing that night when they'd all assembled in her and John's room at the Savoy Hotel to get ready for the evening. Jane does not say anything. She takes the fifth back from John and settles back in her seat, trying to ignore it all.

Mary is also ignoring them all and striding back up 2nd. Without being told to, Jane follows suit, slowly backing up

the street after Mary. Mary is immediately glad to be out of
the car and feel the wind and rain all around him. He walks
faster and faster toward the intersection. The car is just a
yard or two behind him when he suddenly veers left and
runs down Yesler toward 1st Avenue and Puget Sound.
With three cars coming their way, Jane has to idle at the
intersection. When the cars have passed she's still idling,
not sure that it is worth following Mary.

Without looking in either direction Mary scurries across
1st toward the water. At the alley in the middle of the block
before the waterfront Mary ducks in and hurries on north.
He rests in an alley doorway smoking a cigarette, listening
for the sound of his friends pursuing him and watching the
rain splash on the asphalt. By the time his second Lucky
Strike is done he's fairly certain they've lost track of him.

Mary considers working his way up to Capitol Hill and
hiding in one of the bars there.

A way to be alone.

Right now Mary wishes he did not live right across the
street from the neighborhood hangouts.

A third cigarette smoked he decides to turn around and
move back south. He walks under the elevated freeway
viaduct that runs along this end of the waterfront. It rises
a couple of stories over the street but its lower tier keeps the
pavement beneath it drier than the unsheltered sidewalk.

As he walks he loses the morsel of pleasure he'd taken
from telling the others to fuck off.

All he has ever wanted is to be "taken for granted." Taken
for granted on all levels, in every way. He has been very
successful in this with his friends. That's the way he likes it.

To be nothing special. Sometimes he tires of his addiction to Sayyid Husayn.

With Sayyid Husayn he did not really relax, couldn't really enjoy his boyfriend, until the "thrill" was gone. Being with Sayyid Husayn became a pleasure for Mary only after the initial "itch" and "friction" of their lives coming into contact had been overcome. People are always so frantic to maintenance the "thrill" in their relationships and domesticities. But not Mary. Thrills are cheap and temporary; flights-of-fancy, irregularities, freakshows. All those things that create a high degree of agitation. And all this is fake and a fraud to Mary. Something you act out for a john, or some other paying customer.

Where the viaduct slopes back down to join 1st Avenue South Mary stands around for five minutes or so and smokes two more cigarettes. His feet are wet inside his pumps, but with his knee-length gray canvas parka over his blouse and short skirt he's still plenty warm.

He reverses his course and moves north, staying under the viaduct for five or six blocks and then dashing from the viaduct to the loading dock of a building. The loading dock is sheltered from the rain so he decides to sit awhile. He jumps up and sits with his parka tucked underneath his butt and thighs, legs dangling over the edge. Mary smokes cigarettes and kicks the heels of his pumps against the cement of the loading dock.

His back gets tired of being hunched forward. He straightens up and leans back so that his left palm is on the cold cement propping him up. Stretching farther back he twists his neck from side to side, trying to relieve some of the tension. He twists his head to the left and sees that someone is slowly walking toward him along the line of loading docks. Mary cannot tell if it's someone he knows or not. Mary hopes it is a stranger he can abuse and push into a fight. Then he thinks maybe he should leave in case it is one of the crew come to try and cheer him up and cajole him back into the pack.

But he just sits and smokes staring at his shoes. The person gets close enough so he can hear the soles of their shoes scraping the pavement. Mary finally looks to the left again. It is Sayyid Husayn. He squints and stares a second to make sure it isn't an illusion. He looks back at his shoes. Then out toward the Sound.

Mary drags deeply on his Lucky Strike, concentrating on steadying his hands. Cars rumble overhead on the viaduct and the gutters splash and gush water onto the pavement. Sayyid Husayn climbs up onto the loading dock so that he is sitting a couple of feet to Mary's left. Sayyid Husayn looks his boyfriend up and down, making a show of ascertaining that Mary is alright. They both smoke in silence. Mary tosses away his cigarette and glares at his boyfriend.

Mary jumps down and starts walking north. Sayyid Husayn follows after him. The rain is letting up. The streets are wet and cold. When they get to Yesler Way Sayyid Husayn says:

"Let's get a taxi..."

Mary shrugs. They turn right and proceed to 1st Avenue.

8

SPOKANE

They offer their prayers, gifts and desires to a Divinity of their own construction in a basement in Spokane. A deity empowered by desperate needs.

They gathered after school and on weekends in the basement of a boarded-up tavern in a more or less abandoned district on the edge of downtown near where Raeann lives.

On the day the grotto was discovered Raeann and Sheila skipped highschool and spent most of it at Raeann's because both her parents worked. TV got boring so they venture out to wander in alleys and stay out of sight. This particular day they decide to go north. Ending up in this neighborhood of unused warehouses, small empty factories and closed-down cafes and taverns. They spent a good hour going room to room through the three floors of an ex-warehouse.

When Sheila and Raeann exit the warehouse into the alley behind it they find an empty tavern right next door. The door into the actual bar is too tightly sealed to open. But there is a second door. This second door only has a small rusted padlock on it. Using a metal bar they find Sheila and Raeann easily pop the lock off. This door leads down to the basement of the tavern. They swing it open wide and peer into darkness. Dust, mold and maybe something rotting.

Half a dozen cement steps go down into a large storage room. Empty shelves and cardboard liquor boxes. At the rear of this room another door leads farther back under the tavern. This second room had been some sort of office. There's a few metal shelves and a beat-up wooden desk minus one leg and its drawers. There is one last door that is opposite the door leading into the office. The last door opens into a smaller storage room.

Sheila stands in this final doorway, face into the musty darkness saying nothing. After a few minutes Sheila hasn't moved or said anything and Raeann gets a little nervous. She whispers:

"Sheila. Hey, Sheila..."

Sheila looks at her but doesn't say anything. She looks back into the small dark room, digs her Bic lighter out of a jeans' pocket, flicks it and slowly, quietly, walks into this third room. Raeann follows, her own lighter adding its feeble glow to Sheila's.

Sheila walks around the small room, stopping for several minutes in various spots, staring like she is studying something that is being shown to her by someone Raeann does not see.

"This is where we'll wait for Her... and this is where we'll worship... our sneaky little church..."

Raeann thinks the basement is a cool place to explore but she doesn't quite understand what her best friend is talking about.

"What? What are we gonna use this place for?"

Sheila says:

"Come over here, look. We can clean all this up and use

it as our own church. A place to get away to. Somewhere safe, where only our eyes will see what we do..."

She turns and looks directly at Raeann.

"We'll make this the shrine. The secret and holy place.... This is it.... Like we've been needing..."

Raeann is still sort of doubtful.

"Oh, yeah... the shrine thing you've been talking about. But it's so dark and dirty..."

"Yeah yeah, but we can fix it up. And it'll be for us only. This is where we are s'posed to wait for Her to tell us where and when She'll appear..."

Raeann pitches in and they do what rudimentary cleaning they can on their own. After an hour or so they stop. It's time for their friends who went to school to be home.

From a phonebooth they call Harvey. Harvey's 20 and always home. Raeann tries to get across the basic idea of what they've found. Raeann looking periodically at Sheila to make sure she's telling it the way Sheila wants. Harvey gets the general idea and agrees to gather the three other members of their cult.

Raeann goes back to her home to wait for their friends so she can lead them back to the grotto. Sheila stays on and explores the three rooms.

After a while of looking around Sheila doesn't find anything exciting so she goes into the small storage room in back and sits cross-legged on the cement floor. Cool and dank. Occasional scurrying noises of rodents in the tavern overhead. She shifts her body so that she's sitting with her legs bent at the knees and tucked under her.

Sheila starts rocking forward and backward, slowly,

slowly. Back and forth. She fishes her pink Day-Glo rosary out of a jeans' pocket. Sheila starts muttering. A barely audible Rosary rolls across dust and concrete. She rubs the palm of her right hand up and down her blue-jeaned thigh. Her broad face begins to glisten with sweat.

9

Sheila has always been a believer, a feverish believer. Consequently she has never made any effort to believe in Jehovah or Jesus; they've never bothered to come and sit on the edge of her bed at night and comfort her the way the Queen of Angels does.

At eight years of age Sheila starts seeing Our Lady all the time, everywhere. At first only at a distance but over the next two years closer and closer.

Sheila settles into bed and soon She appears and sits with her. Most nights it is a quiet chat until Sheila is able to relax and fall asleep. Some nights there are little mysteries explained to her. Teaching Sheila how to masturbate, all about men (how to stay safe and avoid disease and rugrats), showing her compassion and the marvelous sides of life that are all too often hidden.

There are no divine monologues. They have good full conversations; real back-and-forth exchanges. On Sheila's fifteenth birthday The Lady explains to her that she is an angel given the chance to have a human life, and that soon she will meet other angelic beings in the same circumstances. Once they have all been assembled, Our Lady says She will arrive in the flesh, and on that day of apocalypse the true direction and purpose of their lives will be shown.

It is on a Friday night late in August and the Queen of Angels and Sheila are lying side by side on the bed. Our Lady reveals that within a few weeks Sheila will be meeting some of the other earthbound angels. Sure enough, school starts a couple of weeks later and Sheila meets Raeann Hoyter who is in the same third period English class. It is obvious to Sheila right away that Raeann is another angel. Not long after this she and Raeann befriend four other angels.

10

Raeann, Fred, Harriet, Harvey and Douglas (who is the youngest angel) finally show up at the basement with boxes of cleaning stuff and flashlights. Sheila and Raeann run around pointing and excitedly explaining the main points of the plan. At first the other four are very doubtful. But then they begin to see the potential.

It is decided that they'll leave the main storage room and the office as they are so that if some intruder were to look in from the outer door the place would still appear empty and unused.

"... and back here, in this corner, we'll put the shrine. You know? Like, maybe, on some sort of low platform. You know? Sorta like a stage.

"We can put up strings of those small flashing Christmas lights... and maybe stuff like that little angel on a seashell that I've got. You know, the thing that you plug in and a blue light bulb behind the statue lights up...

"... lots of rugs and pillows and stuff... we'll put candles all around Her... we'll need some blankets... and maybe a cooler for beer and soda and maybe a hot plate for coffee..."

Douglas is wide-eyed, staring into the corner Sheila is trying to describe. Harvey says:

"Yeah... it could be real cool... all sparkling..."

Harvey is 6'4" but he stoops. Though eight inches taller and 80 pounds heavier than Sheila he always deals with her with great deference. He flips his flashlight over to Sheila's face. He hesitates and then says:

"So... what's gonna happen? When do we do all this? And where are we gonna get the electricity... uh, you know..."

This last question makes Sheila pause in her reverie. She turns and looks at him. She tilts her head to the left as if listening to a very quiet voice. After a moment she nods and walks out into the middle office room. Along one wall she kicks aside two cardboard cartons and points to an electrical outlet. The fact that there is this working electrical supply in the basement of this abandoned tavern is considered the second miracle of the grotto. The first being the actual finding of the basement.

The initial arrangement of the icon and its surrounding decorations is rapidly expanded and elaborated on; new trinkets, totems and adornments are found and added. Before long the icon of Our Lady and the platform She rests on is crowded, full of meaning and significant clutter.

The first major event is a series of severe rituals of scarification that has been revealed to Sheila. She oversees this project according to The Lady's instructions. Each of the six of them have a serpent carved into their left buttock. The serpent forms a circle, swallowing its own tail. The first two (on Sheila and Harriet) get infected for a while, but Douglas and Raeann soon get the hang of doing it cleanly.

The central and constantly repeated message of their shrine is that one day when Our Lady of the Ugly Ones, the very Manifestation of the Mystery, will arrive in Spokane. She will appear for them alone. Her appearance will radically and forever change their lives.

A large white piece of cardboard is found and Harriet (who everyone says is real artistic) carefully letters the words "HAIL MARY" on it with a variety of bright Day-Glo paints. Initially the plan was to give the placard decorative borders, but somehow they never get around to it.

Sheila is very concerned that they all remain constantly on the lookout for Her. If, when She appears, they are not looking, carefully scanning, all will be lost. Sheila preaches constant vigilance and full appreciation of all that is going on around them at every minute of the day and night.

11

SEATTLE

The wind rattles the windows in their old and ill-fitting wood frames. Intermittent showers splatter and tap at the glass.

Ring, ring.

Mary jerks awake, stretches, opens his eyes and blinks. They'd left the lamp on the dresser on when they'd lain down. The cassette of Nico they'd fallen asleep to has long since finished.

Ring.

Now Sayyid Husayn stretches, waking up as well. Mary sits up on the bed. It's not quite night yet. Mary can still see the gray clouds in the sky above the three-story buildings across the street.

Mary gets out from under the blankets, stands up and shuffles over to the phone which is next to the lamp on the dresser.

Ring.

"Yes..."

"Mary?! Edith here, dear... what are ya doing?..."

The coy, singsong flippancy of Edith's voice grates ever so slightly. Mary yawns and shivers a second in the evening air.

"Napping. What's up?"

"Well... we're all across the street... Murrow and Ruby are doing shots of Tequila, and as usual, I'm looking at the boys..."

Edith is interrupted by loud voices behind him. Even with the distortion from the phone Mary recognizes one of the voices as Ruby's. Edith covers the mouthpiece with his palm for a moment, then he's back.

"Mary? Okay honey, go over to the window. Uh, the one... on... I think, your... left... yeah it'd be your left..."

Mary sighs and picks up the base of the phone with his right hand. Using a foot he makes sure the cord is free, then he pads over to the formica-topped table in front of the designated window. He sets the body of the phone on the table and picks up a cigarette pack, finds it empty, crumples it and tosses it toward the trashcan. He misses.

"Okay, here I am..."

Mary peers through the drizzle streaks on the glass. He sees the orange and green neon sign of the Frontier Room and the rather small neon cigarette in the single window of Cigarette that passes for its sign.

"Are you looking at the Frontier Room?"

Mary looks closer and sees Jane, Murrow and Ruby in the Frontier Room's big front window. They are obviously looking up in his direction and are waving their arms from side to side in near unison.

"Yeah, yeah... I see'm..."

"Those are *urgent* SOS waves you're seeing there. Please — d'ya hear the pleading tone in my voice? I'm begging — listen, my knees are hitting the filthy linoleum — please, come on over... we're desperate... only you two can possibly save us now..."

Mary turns his head and looks at Sayyid Husayn. He's gathered himself up and is preparing for the evening prayer.

"Sure... yeah okay. We were gonna come over later anyway. So, say, half an hour, 45 minutes?..."

"Groovy!"

Edith turns from the phone and yells to the three at the window.

"He says half an hour, 45 minutes!"

Edith puts the receiver back to his face and says:

"Now Mary, you'd do better to be a little more... mmm... sedate, this evening. There is no fucking way I'm gonna get *this* outfit trashed helping you in some stupid-ass brawl. I'm s'posed to meet this man tonight..."

"A man is meeting you?..."

"Fuck you. Besides, they were gonna 86 those yuppies anyway. There was no real reason for you to cold-cock that jerk."

Mary is irritated at being reminded of the shitheads who'd torn his skirt and bruised his foot last night. He clutches the phone a little tighter.

"Whatever! I didn't see you hesitating to jump right in. And maybe they were fucking *gonna* 86 those pricks... but they let them pollute the place for over an hour and nobody did nothing but "tsk-tsk" when I complained. They need a couple real bouncers in there on Friday and Saturday nights. Oh, whatever.

"That's one good thing about Sunday nights, not so many shitheads around... okay, we'll see you all in a while..."

"Okay.... Oh! Dress up a little. I mean more than usual. There's a party Cheryl Carson is having for her boyfriend. He finally got some gallery to do a show of that Neo-Expressionistic bullshit he does... but Cheryl has been known to have some good parties... sometimes..."

"Sometimes?! Does not sound promising Edith... alright whatever... see ya..."

12

They debate going to this party at all. The debate rages right up to the point Edith is buzzing to get them into the apartment building. Once they are on the right floor they have no trouble finding the party because of the volume of the music inside. They hesitate again standing at the door of 26F. Shuffling their feet and shaking some of the rain off their coats. Looks are exchanged of vague dread.

Murrow gestures and says with exasperation:

"I fucking said it would be like this! Listen to that... Sting! I mean my god."

Mary turns his face away from the door in disgust. Ruby pokes him in the ribs and says:

"Knowing Cheryl we're lucky it's not Guns N' Roses..."

"Guns N' Roses?! Jesuschrist Edith, what the fuck?"

Edith tries to ignore them. He knows there's this one boy that'll be here he's been trying to get know. He starts to bite his lip but stops, not wanting to smear his lipstick or get any on his teeth. He pushes his friends toward the door and has to pound on it quite awhile before anyone hears him and lets them in.

Inside they huddle by the door, scanning the herd and strategizing.

"That's him, over there. The magenta and green hair in the white dinner jacket."

"That's who?"

"Scott, Cheryl's boyfriend. The painter this party's for."

"Hmm."

Ruby shrugs and rolls her eyes.

"Well, I see what looks like the bar back over there, through that doorway. And the food is right over there. I'm going for the eats, then see if I can get a decent dry Martini."

"I... wouldn't count on it, Ruby.... The decent Martini I mean..."

Edith takes off his raincoat and methodically scans the crowd for evidence of the boy.

13

The day had gone well for them. It had been Sayyid Husayn and Mary's turn to handle the wholesale heroin buy this week. A tidy, painless assignment.

Sayyid Husayn couldn't help but smile (among teeth crooked and uneven, yellowed and brown from coffee and tobacco, a single gold tooth glitters) as Eagle Chief's people brought in a cardboard box and took out three bricks of Mexican black tar heroin wrapped snugly in cellophane. His stomach starts churning as soon as he whiffs that chemical smell. Sayyid Husayn doesn't have anything steady going with heroin, but they are definitely on close terms.

Eagle Chief is in an expansive and hospitable mood. She insists both Mary and Sayyid Husayn sit right down and join her for coffee and cookies. Dealing with the Straight Shooters is so much cleaner, safer and friendlier than her experiences with previous Belltown rulers. No more fighting to see who can rip the other off in a bigger way.

A car is waiting for Mary and Sayyid Husayn downstairs and they are driven the few blocks to the front door of the Oregon Hotel. The Straight Shooters have a permanent "lease" on a couple of the hotel's rooms which they use as offices, sleeping rooms, work rooms — whatever.

On this day there are scales, various cutting tools and packaging materials on a table in one of these rooms. Two women and two men are waiting there. It is their job to cut up, weigh out and package the dope for distribution to retailers. For a few minutes Sayyid Husayn and Mary observe their work. The four packagers move through the motions of their duties with such efficiency that the transvestite and the Muslim leave them to it and go look for something else to do.

They stroll down 1st Avenue to the southern edge of Belltown. Standing on the northwest corner of Virginia Street Mary and Sayyid Husayn contemplate the world south of their neighborhood.

Mary looks at Sayyid Husayn, they both shrug and decide to take the chance. They cross the street to the southwest corner and go inside the Virginia Inn for a couple of pints of locally brewed bitters. The Virginia Inn is a favorite of a large clot of the Visual Arts set and an assortment of rockers. But it's early enough in the day to be mostly empty.

They weave their way through the artists and posers gathered for happy-hour pints. Ignoring the walls covered in bad art and the turpentine and pigment banter of the other customers Sayyid Husayn gets them two pints of bitters. They sit side by side at one of the small circular tables, smoking, drinking and watching. After three pints each it's about a quarter to five and the place is filling up fast with after-job drinkers. When these two rockers they don't know want to share their table Sayyid Husayn and Mary look at each other, swig the rest of their bitters as they stand up and push through the crowd to the front door.

Outside, standing under the bar's awning they strain their eyes back up 1st toward the Frontier Room's neon sign. No one. Boarded-over storefronts streaked with rain, graffiti and torn and matted posters and flyers. Too early in the day still. Club Vogue will be starting to serve beer now, but the Vogue wouldn't be any better than what they'd just left. A younger, more pretentious sort is all.

Mary, buzzing on the alcohol, is staring without focus in the general direction of home. Mary is leaning with his weight on the heels of his pumps, swaying slightly from side to side. He is thinking about changing to a fresh piece of chewing gum. The one that's been in his mouth for the last few hours has a distinctly stale beer and cigarette flavor. Sayyid Husayn nudges Mary with an elbow and says:

"Hey, we've come this far, let's go to Left Bank. I need some more magazines."

Mary wheels about and looks south along the 1st Avenue side of the Pike Place Market; dirty, empty shop windows, most boarded over. Mary isn't sure he's up for it. He is thinking of past run-ins he's had in the Market. Mostly with the tourists who persist in roving there despite the continuing deterioration of the chic pastel tourist trap the city had renovated it into a half dozen years ago. It's true the tourists are less thick now as the Market has, for the most part, slumped back into ruination along with the rest of the local economy. But there are still too many tourists, and the police still make a pretense of exerting a medium intensity of law and order. He squints listlessly. He shakes his head no. No, it's just not worth the possible bother.

"Hmm, no. I'm gonna go on home."

Sayyid Husayn is now torn. He hates going into foreign territory unaccompanied. But he really does need some more magazines.

That is a real difference between them. Mary does not read and Sayyid Husayn reads dozens of magazines a week. Left Bank Books and the Market newsstand across the street are the only places downtown that have decent selections of domestic and foreign magazines. And though it's true the Pike Place Market has its own powers-that-be, he's never really had any problems there. Sayyid Husayn makes a practice of psychically ignoring and remaining physically distant from people he does not know. Besides, he's on speaking terms with several of the workers at Left Bank. And being on speaking terms with someone is being friends with that person to Sayyid Husayn. Sayyid Husayn shrugs.

"Okay. I'm gonna take the chance. See you in a couple hours."

They part company. Listen closely and you can hear a slight suction noise as they do so. Two mollusks being pulled apart. Mary crosses Virginia back into the Straight

Shooter security blanket. Sayyid Husayn sets off down
the steep incline of Virginia from 1st to the north end of
Pike Place.

At the northern edge of the Market Sayyid Husayn
pauses, grips his lapels and adjusts the dark brown wool
suit's coat. This motion causes his revolver in its shoulder
holster to rub reassuringly against his chest. Sayyid Husayn
looks up at the sky; cloudy, but rain seems unlikely. He
looks in all directions, then concentrates on his selected
route through the Market. Peeling paint, broken glass, trash,
shattered chips from the brick street that runs through the
Market. He proceeds south.

The Pike Place Market is an L-shape of two long blocks
and one short block. Open-air stalls line both sides of the
street. The buildings are filled with "low end" businesses
and the few tourist traps the traffic will pay for, and garbage
and junk.

Six or so years ago, at the height of its upscale renovation,
the Market had been constantly awash with tourism and
pastel-clothed shoppers. Then when that cycle of prosperity
and growth bottomed out it all devolved back into a jumble
of fish, farm produce and craft stalls, cafes, small groceries,
flea markets, bars, strip joints and drug dealers.

Some of the shops are already closing for the night, but
there are still plenty of people buying, panhandling, loiter-
ing and bartering. Sayyid Husayn walks briskly, face
straight ahead, eyes darting left and right from behind
black-framed ray-bans.

Glance over here, over there. His eyes snap back to the left.
He shakes his head and praises God for having Mary decide

not to come along. Sitting in a semicircle on the sidewalk in front of a boarded-over storefront are six or seven teen-agers. Not just any type of teenagers; all the girls and boys have long wispy hair, several of them with feathers and beads woven in. Everyone in bright tie-dyed tops and bell-bottom blue jeans. One of the young women has a wooden flute which she is playing with an abundance of forced soulfulness. Tooting out a barely recognizable New Age rendition of the Grateful Dead's "Truckin'." One of the boys is holding out a felt hat and trying to keep time with a pair of Hindi finger cymbals. The hat is upside down and the boy shakes it at Sayyid Husayn so that the few coins in it rattle.

Sayyid Husayn is truly relieved Mary is not here. The police do try to keep up a semblance of law and order and if Mary had ended up killing several of these kids it would have been difficult to extricate themselves from the situa-tion. He shakes his head as he walks by. While he does not share the intensity of Mary's hatred of Retro fashions, these kids are particularly dubious and pathetic-looking in their outfits. Sayyid Husayn can't really be bothered one way or the other by the flux of US fashions. A good suit is a good suit, and that is all he wears. Though it's true the narrower the lapel the fonder he is of them. He picks up his pace and scurries past the neo-hippie drek.

Weaving his way along the broken and uneven concrete sidewalk he gradually relaxes and returns to a leisurely scanning of people. As he approaches the south end of Pike Place, right before it meets the short block that begins Pike Street, he starts hearing this loud male voice. Harsh and distorted, haranguing through a bullhorn. Sayyid Husayn stops and considers going back home. But he pushes ahead to the corner and on around it.

Sure enough. On the sidewalk outside Left Bank Books near the intersection of 1st and Pike there are three evangelists. Judging from their attire, the tabloid they're hawking and their rant Sayyid Husayn figures them for Maoist evangelists. The man with the bullhorn is chanting a cycle of Marxist-Leninist litanies and waving a copy of the Revolutionary Worker at passers-by. He is flanked by two junior party hacks, each clutching the same tabloid along one edge so that the garish headlines and lurid cover illustrations are clear for all to see. All three are dressed in the standard part outfit. US Army Surplus olive-drab jackets, blue jeans and pseudo-Punk haircuts.

Sayyid Husayn falters. He tries to scuttle by the Communists without meeting their gaze and make it into the bookstore. But the toe of his left shoe catches on an uneven slab of sidewalk, and he stumbles. This is all the opening the Maoist with the bullhorn needs. The Party cadre almost leaps in front of Sayyid Husayn.

Spittle flying from his lips he feverishly recites and coughs up the prescribed Maoist formulas. The man's eyes are wide and red. His mouth is opening, opening, opening, tongue slashing out the words. Sayyid Husayn cannot take his eyes off the mouth and the tongue. For 60 seconds Sayyid Husayn is frozen. Then he shoves the man in the gut and dashes into Left Bank.

Once safely inside he wipes the sweat from his face with his handkerchief. The guy behind the counter smiles slyly and says:

"Hey there Husayn."

The shop clerk glances out the window at the Communist who is now staring in at Sayyid Husayn, his mouth still working away. The man at the cash register smiles again.

"Pretty scary huh."

Sayyid Husayn puts away his handkerchief, shakes his head, smiles uneasily and gets out his cigarettes.

14

Mary is a 31-year-old man with a revolver in a cheap cotton dress.

He only occasionally forgets this. His world view and all his actions emanate from this circumstance and apparel.

Mary is not a vigilante. He is not against criminals, victimizers or thugs. He is one. Though he does hold to the opinion that white-collar criminals do not really do an honest day's work for their share of the spoils.

Mary never has doubts, or hesitations, about what is "just" or "right" as something is happening or is told to him. There is no duty or program.

Sayyid Husayn is different. Sayyid Husayn has faith. He too has a side arm. But he wears suits and has surrendered to God.

Death is not his worry. It is the potential for him to be tortured again that causes him to fire round after round into the darkness.

Despite his readiness to shoot first Sayyid Husayn keeps

in mind a certain saying, attributed to the sainted and incomparable Mulla Nasr ud-Din.

"Steady and sure the finger on the trigger, because quick and firm the body to the grave."

15

Mary was The Dictator's last mistress. They became acquainted while Mary was tending bar at a place near the Greyhound depot called De Ville's. De Ville's was a hangout for various criminal cliques and crews from different parts of Seattle, as well as a multitude of wannabes.

One of the larger (and poorer-tipping) posses to use De Ville's as a clubhouse were the Fiances of Death. A mostly south Seattle operation that controlled the redlight strip down near SeaTac Airport. Not a big mover-and-shaker type of setup, but it provided a steady income and a firm power base.

The boss was a man named George Burwell — The Dictator. He fancied himself a sort of latter-day little Hitler. It was he who latched onto the moniker "Fiances of Death," first used by a deathsquad in Bolivia run by this "retired" Gestapo officer, Klaus Barbie. The phrase "Fiances of Death" had leapt up off the pages of Time magazine at Burwell; he was instantly enamored of it.

The Dictator held court in one of the large back booths at De Ville's. When not in use by him and his posse the booth was partitioned off with a black ribbon like a half dozen other booths kept in reserve for clients who could pay the price.

Mary supervised the bar and rigidly enforced the cocktail lounge's neutrality. Thus rival criminal organizations, and even certain law enforcement officials (particularly the special "anti-drug" cops), could belly up to the bar, receive a complimentary drink, and not have to notice who their drinking companions were.

Mary treated them all with equal disinterest and contempt. He made a special point of ignoring the wormy peons scuttling from booth to booth, running messages, fetching drinks and food and generally doing anything they thought might earn them the brownie points needed to sit in the boss's booths.

The epithet "The Dictator" was originated by the prostitutes Burwell's boys managed. At first it was only spoken in a vicious whisper among the whores. Then their immediate supervisors and some of the footsoldiers began using it with one another. In respectful and fearful tones. But soon the name worked its way up the power chain.

One night after a late dinner at De Ville's and a lot of booze Burwell is relishing a lieutenant's report on a particularly nasty bit of enforcement work. This item on his agenda finished, he asks for a report on recent rumblings and minor revolts within his stable of women and boys. The lieutenant who is called on to give this report has had several more drinks than is advisable for a man who must keep his wits and cool about him. He blusters and rails against the faggots and queens in the posse's employ because they have joined the group of women who are staging a work slowdown.

"Those cocksuckers are the shits who started refusing to screw the guys they don't *like* for christsake. It was that kid Murphy that said, 'The Dictator can sleep with this asshole if he needs the money so fucking... '... uh..."

He seizes up and stops talking. He flushes red and then goes completely pale. His lips move but all the words he can think of to say will not retract his having said that name out loud. The name they all use, but have been careful never to speak in Burwell's presence. The man shrinks back in the booth, coughs like he is gagging and turns an ill green.

The Dictator stares at this man, then around the table at his other lieutenants. From the variety of reactions on their faces it is apparent they have all heard this name before. Use it themselves most likely. He leans back and thinks about it a minute or two. His face is as thoughtful as he is capable of. In one gulp he downs the rest of his Whiskey Sour and reaches into his suit for his Walther 9mm automatic in its shoulder holster. The men sitting on either side scramble to get away from their associate who has been so indiscreet. The Dictator grins. Gun in hand he pushes his way out of the booth. Standing in front of it he shifts his attention from his own men to the rest of the lounge. He has a big grin and his pistol pointed to the ceiling.

"You all better fucking believe it! I *am* The Dictator! The Dictator of Love!"

It is in this way that "The Dictator" became an open and public term of respect and loyalty.

That The Dictator regularly fucked Mary in an ugly little box of an apartment in the northern residential zone of Seattle remained a secret while it was happening. It was not the sort of thing either of them wanted anyone else to know about, but for somewhat different reasons.

It didn't happen right away. Mary worked De Ville's for more than a year before The Dictator made any move on him. In fact, The Dictator's attitude toward Mary shifted between ignoring and insulting him.

One night the place is really packed and Mary has to wait on a few tables plus tend bar. Burwell actually pays for a round of drinks for his table. He hands Mary a 50-dollar bill folded in half. When Mary unfolds it back at the cash register he finds a small torn corner of paper with a date, time and address on it, penciled in tiny numbers and letters. Mary stands there a second holding the piece of paper and looking over his shoulder in The Dictator's direction. He considers taking the Mac-10 from under the bar and shooting Burwell right then and there. But he doesn't. Mary returns the change, pockets the meager tip and then walks away, paying no attention to The Dictator.

In the next several days leading up to the appointed hour Mary vacillates about showing up. The day before the "date" he finally decides to go through with it. Once he's made up his own mind he confides his plans to Sayyid Husayn, Ruby and Edith. Ruby is of course dead set against it. The Straight Shooters are not entirely secure yet and Ruby doesn't like the idea of any of her people becoming entangled with a larger and more powerful gang. Edith is thrilled and even sort of jealous (again) of his cousin.

Sayyid Husayn rolls his eyes, beseeches God and the Shaykha ("Elder") for guidance and peace and thanks Mary for letting him in on it all before it happens. All he and Ruby ask for is a phone call as soon as Mary's out of there.

So Mary takes a taxi way up to the northern edge of the city's suburbs. Beyond any part of Seattle he's ever bothered to go to. The address turns out to be a dreary modernistic apartment complex.

Mary pauses for one heartbeat at the fake wood door of #33. He glances back down the corridor. The man he figures is the manager is no longer following him. He adjusts his skirt and knocks twice.

Mary is not very surprised that The Dictator is alone. No three or four bodyguards, nothing. Mary sorta figured it'd be this way. What with Burwell's super-macho pose and his image of control. Burwell wouldn't want to disillusion all the little boys who look up to him. Maybe they wouldn't want to understand that he is all the more of a stud because he does occasionally enjoy fucking a bit of boypussy. It was perhaps an acquired taste, which he had several years to cultivate during a couple of stretches in the Federal prison at Walla Walla. And besides, Mary wears a skirt doesn't he? It does surprise Mary though that The Dictator didn't even check him for weapons.

The "love nest" apartment is at least as hideous on the inside as the building was on the outside. Semi-gloss white walls and sparkling spackled ceilings. A brown semi-shag floor covering everywhere except the bathroom. A couch and one easy chair covered in the same beige fake fur. The bedroom is as sparse and undecorated as the rest of the place. Only a bed and dresser.

Mary refuses to even touch, let alone sit on, the fake fur. He hands The Dictator his parka and walks into the bedroom.

Mary undresses and drapes his clothes on top of the dresser. He lies down on the bedspread on his stomach. The Dictator stands alongside the bed and stares at Mary's shoulder-length blonde hair and his ivory white, sharply muscled body. The Dictator stares at a series of scars crisscrossing Mary's upper thighs and buttocks. The Dictator slurps at his Canadian whisky and then says:

"Here, look at this."

Mary turns over and sits up. Burwell opens the room's closet door and points a thick finger circled in a fat gold band at an ankle-length black leather coat hanging inside. He reaches down and picks up two pairs of expensive-looking pumps, he then pulls a 50-dollar bill from his slacks' pocket and stuffs it into the toe of one of the shoes.

The Dictator is not tall. He is not very muscled. He is sort of fat. Only one usable eye and a variety of scars on his face and squat torso.

The Dictator fucks Mary like he is digging a ditch. He orgasms choking and slobbering on the back of Mary's neck. When finished he remains lying on him, crushing down on him. He starts whispering and grunting about how repulsive he finds Mary, and how he'd never, ever be seen in public with Mary like he would a woman. Thankgod for some things Mary thinks. Mary lies beneath Burwell saying nothing. The Dictator dirty-talks himself into another hard-on, lubricates himself again and goes back to plowing.

When The Dictator finally gets up and showers Mary swiftly dresses, smokes a cigarette and examines the coat in the closet. Deciding it is real leather he rolls it up and stuffs it and the shoes into a large plastic shopping bag Burwell's left on the closet floor. Mary goes into the living room, puts on his parka, sets the bag of stuff on the floor next to the easy chair.

It is on this first date that Mary decides to use these rendezvous' to find an opportunity to kill Burwell. Not right away. In a couple months. Before word of their boss's fling leaks to the rest of the Fiances, or Burwell decides to try and kill him first. It would be soon enough so that no one knows it was him that snuffed the shithead.

The Dictator comes out of the bathroom toweling his hair. When he sees Mary he grimaces and gestures for him to leave. Mary grabs his purse and the bag full of stuff and swaggers to the door. Without turning he says:

"Again?..."

"You want it again faggot?"

Mary doesn't reply, he just stands there.

"Yeah, sure you do... I'll let you know..."

At least once a week, and sometimes twice, for four months they met in the same apartment. When at De Ville's they kept to the same act as before anything had happened. Actually, The Dictator increases the level of verbal abuse he dishes Mary. Mary never says anything at all. He accumulates plenty of stuff.

The Dictator never varies his circus at De Ville's. He loves an audience. One or two nights a month The Dictator and his boys bring in a 12-, 13-, *maybe* 14-year-old girl who is new to their stable. For the first couple of hours she's all excited. Thrilled at being privileged to sit in The Dictator's booth. All the attention, the food, liquor and drugs make her feel special.

Once he has his dinner and several drinks The Dictator starts the warm-up event of the evening's show. First, he makes a big production of taking off the girl's under-wear and waving it around over his head. Next she is made to sit on various laps and get thoroughly groped. Maybe she starts getting uncomfortable, or even a little scared, but whispered threats of a bullwhip keep her in line. Then The Dictator gets out a tube of very red lipstick that he always carries for these occasions. With great care and soft cooing words he applies it to the girl's lips. This is the prelude to the main act.

She is made to crawl under the table and crouch between The Dictator's knees. At this point he leans back in his seat so that his lieutenants and honored guests can watch. He smiles and then real fatherly-like tells her to unzip his slacks and give him a blowjob. He always likes a fresh drink at hand to sip while the girl works his ugly, rarely washed penis.

If The Dictator is in a particularly magnanimous mood that evening the girl is forced to orally service a few of his favored companions. Once she's finished her assignments she is allowed to sit back up with them. She is not allowed to go to the bathroom to insure that she's swallowed their sperm, and because Burwell likes to see them with the red lipstick all smeary on their lips and faces.

Mary watches it all and thinks about entrance and exit wounds produced by a .38 fired at close range. He is glad it is not his lips around Burwell's ugly dick in front of that audience.

"You stupid pathetic fucking faggot. You'd love it if I took you out with me some night and showed you off... so that everyone could see that you had a *man* fucking you. I know all about you shiteating cocksuckers..."

"What would I want that for? So I can suck you off from under a table?..."

The Dictator stops on his way to the shower. He looks back at Mary with a nasty, hateful glower. He snorts derisively and points a forefinger at Mary like it is a pistol. Mary watches him walk away.

Mary dresses quickly and packs his presents as usual. He sets the bag of stuff to the right of the apartment's front door. He takes his revolver, still in its shoulder holster, from his handbag and straps it back on under his left arm. He puts on his parka, unholsters the Smith & Wesson and attaches a silencer.

The bathroom door is not locked. Mary counts to 10 and steps to the drawn aqua shower curtain. Burwell's body is square in the middle of the stall. Gripping the pistol with both hands Mary fires twice. Burwell crashes to the tiled floor of the stall. Mary yanks aside the curtain, moves one step back to avoid any splashing water and shoots Burwell in the head two more times for good measure. One of the bullets hits the floor at such an angle and velocity as to send pieces of lead hurling into the ceiling. Mary goes back to the living room and smokes two cigarettes. As he smokes the second one he moves around the apartment wiping down the few smooth surfaces he's let himself touch. This takes about 10 minutes when done at a leisurely pace. Then he goes back into the bathroom to make sure The Dictator is dead. He is, but it pays to make absolutely sure with a guy like Burwell.

16

The manager of the apartment complex is very reluctant to enter #33 even though water is pouring through the ceiling into #23. The Dictator made special arrangements with Gene regarding #33. Assumed name, no questions asked, 12 months in advance, and another crisp 100-dollar bill in the manager's pocket each month. And Burwell's made it very clear he never under any circumstance is to be disturbed when he's inside #33.

Finally, sweating bullets, Gene lets himself in and finds the body crumpled in the shower. White, bloodless, blocking the drain and causing the flooding into the lower apartment. Gene stares, the water lapping at his loafers. He shuts off the taps, then leaves the apartment, locking it behind him. Gene does not bother to collect all his personal possessions, let alone call the police. He understood quite well who Burwell was. Gene stuffs a few things into a gym bag. He withdraws as much money as he can from a cashmachine and gets on a Greyhound for Portland, Oregon.

It is four days before an Assistant City Prosecutor, friendly with the Fiances, is able to find out that the Seattle Police Department has hidden Burwell's body. The cops are trying to keep it to themselves as long as possible to use their knowledge to its fullest PR advantage.

Gene is pretty sure he knows who did it. Not only does Gene know who Burwell was, but he also knows all about what Burwell did in this apartment, and with whom. Just for a lark The Dictator had him install a small video camera in the ceiling of the bedroom to tape a few of the love scenes. Afterwards Gene and Burwell would go back to Gene's apartment and review the tapes over Vodkas. When he left his apartment that last time Gene took the two videocassettes with him.

Gene spends the next four years working various jobs and living with his sister and brother-in-law. Four years and he is broke and bored. Four years and still no one has ever come up with The Dictator's killer. So Gene starts to wondering if maybe there could be some money in putting the two videos into Fiance hands. He finally spills the details to his sister and brother-in-law. They agree there could be a fair hunk of quick and easy money via the videos. The three of them drive up to Seattle and check into the Beauview Motel near SeaTac Airport.

A few days of spending time in bars along the SeaTac strip, hinting around in the right ears, and word finally makes it up the vine to the clique of The Dictator's lieutenants who came to dominate the Fiances of Death. One night soon after there is a knock knock at the motel room door and Gene, his sister and her husband are made stars in a snuff film.

It takes the Fiances another couple of weeks to figure out the identity of the other man in the videos. For the sake of their own power base, and for the sake of The Dictator's reputation, the ruling clique evolves a story whereby this dragqueen somehow induced The Dictator to service him. All strictly against Burwell's will. They are eager to believe this themselves and it further motivates their masculine urges to avenge the honor of a great man and a great heterosexual. Most of the organization's new projects are put on hold and resources concentrated on finding this dragqueen.

After killing Burwell Mary is pretty sure he got away with it. Even so he gradually quits working De Ville's. Not so suddenly as to draw attention, but long before his bored face is revealed to the Fiances in the videos.

   Years go by and Mary feels safe. The Straight Shooters are secure in their own power base and Belltown feels fortified and invincible. But then rumors start circulating, creeping around, that the Fiances may have finally ID'd Mary.

17

BEIRUT–PARIS–NEW YORK CITY

Mary works at avoiding implications. Like electrodes applied too vigorously and too frequently to Sayyid Husayn's
tits by Christian militiamen in Beirut. Implication – a mat
of scar tissue instead of a left nipple.

When they'd tortured Sayyid Husayn "long enough" they
dumped him in an abandoned monastery being used as a
prisoncamp for rival militias, most of whom were Muslims.
The prisoners from Sidon, where Sayyid Husayn's family
live, and specifically the other prisoners from his clan and
the militia they all belonged to tried to incorporate him into
their fold. But at age 14 Sayyid Husayn Masur had no more
interest in anything like civil wars.

Sayyid Husayn keeps to himself. Off to one side
praying and beseeching the Messenger Muhammad
(peace be upon him – pbuh), the Household of the
Messenger (peace be upon them – pbut) and the blessed
Imams (pbut). The rest of his days are spent trying to stay
out of the embraces of the guards and the clutches of the
Masur clansmen prisoners. (He spends as much time as
he can up in one of the ruined church steeples looking
out at the blue Mediterranean.)

Some weeks pass in this way and then Sayyid Husayn
becomes attached to another solitary youth by the name of
Rashid. Rashid had been studying toward initiation into the

upper levels of one of the Sufi orders before his older brothers and father had pressed him into joining them in the militia the family supported. Through this young man Sayyid Husayn undergoes a major reordering of his spiritual affiliations. Initially with fear and guilt he switches his religious allegiance from mainstream Twelver Shi'ia and the earthly deputies of the Hidden Imam (pbuh), who his clan has adored for hundreds of years, to that of the much more obscure and mysterious Qiyamati Ismaili sect. Considered extremist and heretical, the Qiyamati Ismaili are guided by the now-aged daughter of the previous Elder. Always on Rashid's person is a tattered black-and-white photo of this woman, seated on a rug, one arm resting on a low circular wooden table with several books open on it. Her eyes intense and staring.

After several particularly lengthy and intensive beatings the guards dump Rashid in the dirt courtyard. Blood seeping steadily from several injuries to his skull. Sayyid Husayn cannot get him to wake up. For two days Sayyid Husayn remains at Rashid's side administering what care he can. When Rashid dies Sayyid Husayn removes a leather pouch from around his companion's neck. In the pouch is the snapshot of Hajja Shaykha Sayyida Zaynab Batin. From now on this photo is always either on his person or tacked up where he is living on the wall facing Mecca.

Not long after Rashid's death another boy takes an interest in Sayyid Husayn. He is a 19-year-old Lebanese Circassian named Rustam Ashkari. Rustam is the boss of a group of streetboys the Christian militia had rounded up as a part of their periodic efforts to curb crime. Rustam makes sure Sayyid Husayn eats and keeps him away from the older prisoners and guards who either exchange food for sexual favors or just take take them as they like. It is Rustam who seduces Sayyid Husayn back into living.

Months pass and the Christian militia decide it is politically expedient to empty the prisoncamp of the younger prisoners in preparation for a Red Cross tour of prison facilities in the Christian zone of Beirut. Sayyid Husayn decides to stay on with Rustam and his crew. For one thing the Masur clan know he is out on the streets and Sayyid Husayn's father has given orders for him to be captured and returned to the family's control. So it is safer if Sayyid Husayn spends most of his time inside the apartment the gang uses as its base and dormitory.

Rustam and his people get involved in a very lucrative business doing a freelance bodyguard thing for the intermediaries between those who raid militia depots and those who sell stolen materiel on the gray and black markets. This lasts almost a year.

In the meantime Sayyid Husayn's father, Sayyid Abd' ul-Lah Masur, is released from another prisoncamp. Back in public, the family patriarch is faced with dealing with the public humiliation of Sayyid Husayn having rejected not only the Masur family, and the militia to which the entire clan adhere to, but his breaking of the family's religious heritage. And then to go and live in the company of such disruptive, antisocial elements.

Straight out of his confinement Sayyid Husayn's father runs to see the family's one powerful relative. Uncle Lutif is more than happy to garner a debt to another part of the clan. He eagerly grants his assistance in getting back the wayward son.

Right around dawn one spring morning nine heavily armed men in Uncle Lutif's employ dispatch the boy on watch in the hall of the posse's apartment building and smash through the apartment's door. Rustam and Sayyid Husayn are curled up asleep in a corner, a half dozen other kids are sleeping elsewhere in the apartment. None of the sleeping occupants is given the chance to surrender. There is no time to offer anything but a half-assed defense. Machineguns are spitting and shredding. Blood is pouring from several holes in Rustam's chest, Sayyid Husayn fumbles with his revolver. Two of the raiders tackle him and jab a hypodermic needle into his arm.

The Masurs use favors and cash in the right hands to get a heavily sedated Sayyid Husayn onto a boat to Cyprus and then a corporate plane to Paris where the family has relatives.

It is all decided. Sayyid Husayn will live in Paris and get rehabilitated and educated so he can be married off. A couple of months in isolation and regular beatings and the patriarch of his cousins' family decides Sayyid Husayn's spirit is broken enough that they can start sending him to an exclusive Muslim private school for boys. For several months Sayyid Husayn is closely watched and monitored by the family and school administration.

Sayyid Husayn opts for obedience and conformity as the best method to help get him room to maneuver and escape. Self-delusion on the part of the familial authorities leads to gaps in the security net big enough for Sayyid Husayn to polka through. Once his French is passable he does just that. He spends a lot of time turning tricks in a public men's room in one of the busier Metro stations. Gradually he accumulates a nice stash of francs.

Summer comes around again and Sayyid Husayn has a plan. So a few days before the summer break begins he skips his last two classes and works a men's lavatory he's previously found profitable. He turns down all advances until he comes across a Belgian punter whose wallet is lush with cash. With the Belgian's trousers around his ankles and his penis in Sayyid Husayn's mouth the man is oblivious to his wallet being plundered. This money plus what Sayyid Husayn's already saved is plenty to make a start.

As Sayyid Husayn hurries out of the public convenience he rubs the palms of his hands up and down the front of the suit coat he has on. One of these hands feels the wad of cash and the other his passport, taken that morning from where the family patriarch had hidden it. Sayyid Husayn praises God, the Messenger Muhammad (pbuh) and the Elder. Sayyid Husayn is ready to go.

Sayyid Husayn wipes his mouth again and looks around for a newsstand to buy some chewing gum to mask the residual flavor of the Belgian's sperm. Something like Clorox and an ashtray. There's nothing in the area. Sayyid Husayn lights a cigarette and hails a taxi for Orly Airport. He can pick up some chewing gum there before whatever flight he finally decides to get on.

At the airport he stands looking at the electronic board announcing departing flights for the next six or so hours. He picks out a direct flight to New York City leaving in an hour and a half. On his way to one of the airport's cocktail lounges Sayyid Husayn purchases a package of Wrigley's Doublemint chewing gum.

Sayyid Husayn lives in a residential hotel on the far western side of midtown Manhattan. Initially he just lives on his savings and gorges on TV and smokes cigarettes. He uses the TV to learn and sharpen his English. When the money runs down he goes back to the streets for his living.

Once his savings run out Sayyid Husayn goes to work on the streets of lower Manhattan. Keeping himself separate from the other boys he stakes out a small stretch of sidewalk along the Hudson River and tries to sift through the shoppers.

He figures out how many men at what price he needs to pay the rent, the rest is all savings and pocket money. Once he has a reasonable roll of money he goes out and buys himself a good pistol and shoulder holster. A nice Colt .38 revolver with a three-inch barrel. Just right for close-in problems. Blued black with a crisscross grip to steady things when he sweats, which he does a lot. This tool inside his coat Sayyid Husayn goes with men to their homes and robs them if they are well-off.

Manhattan is alright, but Sayyid Husayn is restless. He does not feel like staying here for much longer. Returning to Beirut or even Europe seems unlikely.

Months go by and now Sayyid Husayn is 17. The more he learns about the western United States the stronger it appeals to him. He realizes there are no longer indigenous nomadic tribes out there that he can join. But he is entranced by the frenzied media reports about raging gang warfare on the West Coast.

In the Mid-Manhattan branch of the New York Public Library Sayyid Husayn studies a map of the United States and decides on San Francisco, California, next.

18

SAN FRANCISCO

Sayyid Husayn wakes up slowly. He sits up and looks around. Something is wrong. There is too much light coming in through the thin white nylon curtains. He looks at his wristwatch on the side table. Nine o'clock. He double-checks that the PM is displayed on the watch face. It is. He listens carefully. Nothing. In fact, too much nothing. Where are the sounds from the street three stories down?

Sayyid Husayn gets his revolver and tiptoes to the door. He stands there in his boxer shorts and T-shirt, ear to the door, hand ready to release the Colt's safety catch. Nothing in the hallway. To be sure he crouches down to look through the narrow gap between the door and the carpet. He stands and leans against the door. He looks over at the drawn white curtains. He is sure it is lighter than it should be out there.

Sayyid Husayn goes quietly to the bed, sets the revolver on it, and never taking his eyes off the curtains steps into a pair of slacks.

At the curtains he pauses and listens. The street sounds are very muffled. He peeks through the gap in the fabric. He draws the left curtain aside a few inches. Outside the air is filled with what looks like dense smoke. He panics and thinks there must be an enormous fire, perhaps on one of the lower floors. But there are no sirens or shouting, no smell of smoke.

He opens the window a crack and sticks his nose up to it. He draws a deep breath. Very cold and damp. Ugh. Fog. For a couple of moments it's intriguing. He opens the window all the way. Down on the street a few neon signs and streetlights are a dim glow.

He eventually leaves the window and shaves at the mirror over the room's sink. He can't decide if he should go outside anyway or wait for it to go away. He worries about how he will maintain a useful visual defensive perimeter if he can't see from corner to corner of a block.

He sets out a suit, white shirt and tie, polishes his shoes and sets the small steel espresso pot to boil on the room's hot plate. In clean boxers and T-shirt he carries out the evening prayer.

For several minutes (definitely more than five) Sayyid Husayn stands in the entryway to his hotel in the Tenderloin. He is able to pass through the first set of double doors effortlessly, but stops dead at the outer set. He passes a few minutes messing with his hair and adjusting his tie. Finally he turns and faces the outer doors again. He strains to see out into the fog.

Sayyid Husayn adjusts his topcoat as a discreet way of reassuring himself that his revolver is indeed there in its shoulder holster.

Leaning on the left door he shoves it open a foot or so. Outside the night air is wet, cold and stifled. He cannot clearly hear the city's soundtrack. It is cold but Sayyid Husayn is sweating a little. He berates himself for this fear and pushes the door all the way open and steps out into the deeply cloaked night. He can see only a few yards ahead and keeps next to the buildings. Who's to say what people and other dangers lie beyond this field of vision. He walks slowly, trying to be casual and not to look like he's skulking. It's not long after this that he starts planning to leave this city.

One morning a month or so later Sayyid Husayn wakes up in a stranger's bed. This is not surprising. He spends a great deal of time in certain districts – the Castro, North Beach, the Mission; and especially the one he lives in, the Tenderloin – turning tricks or just getting picked up by men he thinks might have something at home worth stealing. Last night it was North Beach. Nothing going on most of the night and then there was this man. They'd gone drinking and finally he'd gotten drunk enough to ask Sayyid Husayn home for the night.

Sayyid Husayn has a series of stories worked up for the various situations he finds himself in to explain his carrying a gun. More often than not once they decide he is not going to kill them the men find the fact that he does pack a revolver rather erotic.

Sayyid Husayn has found it easiest to play the "Ignorant Foreigner" – shy, naive and lonely – with most of the men he goes home with. Unless it's an outright paying job. Men who pay like him to be tougher and even hostile. It makes them feel like they are getting to screw a straight boy who would not ordinarily go in for such activities.

This morning the stranger whose bed he is in has already gone off to work. There is a cute note for him on the kitchen table. This note is written in large block printing, as if this makes it easier for someone the writer believes cannot understand much English. It asks if Sayyid Husayn will be there when the man gets off work, or at least leave a phone number. Sayyid Husayn incinerates this piece of paper in the microwave.

Sayyid Husayn has coffee and rummages through the man's apartment. There's some cash, but far more interesting is an airline ticket to Seattle, Washington. Sayyid Husayn is pretty sure that Seattle is a city on the West Coast as well.

He looks at his watch. Almost 11am. Time to get going. This guy is the kind who just might decide to come home during his lunch hour to see if Sayyid Husayn is still there. Sayyid Husayn puts the airline ticket in the inside pocket of his suit coat, next to the photo of the Elder, and leaves.

There are three more days paid up on his hotel room, but Sayyid Husayn packs his shoulder bag and his garment bag and leaves without bothering to check out.

Sayyid Husayn is excited to be on the move again. He rides the bus out to San Francisco International Airport plugged into his walkman, listening to the tremulous tones of the little Turkish boy, Kuchuk Emrah, who had been Rustam's favorite singer. It costs him $40.00 to get the stolen ticket exchanged for one usable on a flight that afternoon.

19

SEATTLE

The table is rectangular and rounded at the corners. One of the ends (the one where the formica top is most cracked and chipped) is pushed up against the wall of the hotel room facing 1st Avenue. Directly above this end of the table is the sill of the window in the left half of the wall (if you are facing the street).

The formica top is a low-gloss olive color with no pattern in it. The formica is held down at the edges by a relatively shiny band of chrome which encircles the rim of the table. This band of chrome is probably more than two inches wide. The surface dimensions of the table are probably two and a half feet on the ends and maybe five and a half feet or so on the sides.

On the end closest to the windows are an old chrome toaster and a yellow paisley-shaped ceramic ashtray. There is also a tall souvenir drinking glass from the Seattle World's Fair of 1962. A few pieces of silverware rest in it. There are a couple of other things at that end of the table.

At the opposite end (pointing to the room's door) is a red paisley-shaped ceramic ashtray. A filterless Lucky Strike smolders in one of the ashtray's fluted slots. To the left of the ashtray are three or four coffee stains. All uneven circles randomly intersecting each other. Very near these is a large coffee mug. Steam rises from the coffee and milk. To the far left of these things is a pack of Lucky Strikes and a rectangular steel Zippo lighter. Cigarette and coffee — a whore's breakfast.

The left side of the table is six or so inches from the wall. Along the right side are two chrome and vinyl kitchen-type chairs. At the end of the table, near the coffee and ashtray, is a third chair of the same materials. Of the three chairs only two are of the same design.

More to the middle of the table is a disassembled revolver and the tools to clean and oil it. The revolver is Mary's favorite, a Smith & Wesson .38 he's had for years.

It is late morning. The sky is overcast, the room's overhead lights are all on. It's warm enough outside that both the windows are ajar a couple of inches. A slight breeze pushes its way into the room in gusts. Depending on the direction of the wind (such as today from the west and northwest) the smells of Puget Sound filter into the room.

The sky is dark gray, but it is not raining at the moment. The windows face west, toward the Sound. You cannot see the Sound though. All that is visible are the cloudy sky and the three-story buildings across the street. These buildings are of the same style as the Strand Hotel. The Frontier Room and Cigarette occupy the ground floor of one of them. Taking up the 2nd and 3rd floors is the Oregon Hotel. Another cheap, by-the-day or by-the-week, close-to-slummy residential hotel. Looking on the inside very much like this room at the Strand.

The chair in front of the ashtray, coffee and cigarette is pushed back from the table a couple of feet. Mary has gone to put another cassette in the boombox.

Not used to being awake at a little after 10 in the morning Mary can't decide if he should eat some food or what. Once he has The Birthday Party in the box and at a suitable volume Mary walks back to the table and stands there looking from coffee to cigarette to dismantled revolver. He decides that just one mug of coffee and milk is not going to be enough.

He shuffles over to the room's kitchenette counter, empties the medium-size steel espresso pot, refills it with fresh water and finely ground coffee. Once it's set up and resting on one of the two gas burners of the half-size stove (no oven) Mary lights the gas and goes back to the table. He picks up the coffee mug and finishes off the first round.

Traffic comes and goes along 1st Avenue. Will Sayyid Husayn be home on the 11am or noon Greyhound from Portland? He has spent four days with Mary's mother and grandmother. At this point in Mary and Sayyid Husayn's lives Mary's mom and grandma function more as Sayyid Husayn's parents than his.

Mary snubs out the cigarette, sits down and scoots the chair forward till his abdomen is an inch or so from the rim of the table. He sits and stares out the window, rubbing the place on the side of the middle finger of his right hand where years of smoking filterless cigarettes has built up a dime-size patch of yellow, calloused skin. He shoves the red ashtray farther to the left and pulls the pistol and cleaning tools forward. He hums along with Nick Cave. He draws a bit of cloth through the barrel and each of the six chambers of the cylinder a few times. This done he lights another Lucky Strike. The coffee pot is starting to hiss and gurgle.

As he stands up to attend to it Mary stubs his toes on the table leg on his right. He grimaces and limps slightly over to the stove.

Mary has kicked the northeast table leg. The impact of flesh on metal causes three cockroaches on the floor near this table leg, busy communicating with every means available to them, to dash off in three different directions. By the time Mary has refilled his mug with brackish black coffee, added the milk and is settled down at the table (legs crossed at the knee), the insects are safely hidden in various roach observation points beneath ledges and the baseboard.

20

Sayyid Husayn goes through phases. One month he's all itchy-twitchy about pert creases and smoothly pressed suits. A couple of months later the collars of his white shirts are gray and yellowed, the suits are slept in and the slacks have tears in them. In these periods he completely abandons the use of ties of any sort.

Those periods when he wants his clothes clean and pressed do not correspond with an inner sense of cleanliness and crispness. Quite the opposite.

When the nightmares are clocking in one after the other, night after vivid night, when there is little else in his life but anxiety and panic – there is his appearance. Well, there is God, and there is Mary. But it is his look – neat and precise – that holds his personality in place. There is great comfort for him in the precise administration of appearance. And because appearance is most valuable to him in a public context he spends these episodes 24 hours a day in pursuit of social settings.

The pleasure is in exhibitionism. Beauty is in the eye of the wearer. Possibly in the eye of the beholder, but not necessarily.

21

Mary has taken the time to change clothes. Dressing up a little more than he does most nights. Makeup's on, skirt, sweater, a bit of Windex to sharpen the shine on a pair of black patent leather pumps.

But Mary is fidgeting. He sits at the table and smokes another cigarette. He gets a craving to a hear a particular song and digs around in the shoe boxes full of cassettes and the heap of tapes next to the bed until he finds the one with Joy Division on both sides. New cassette playing he reapplies his lipstick in a different shade of red. He studies himself in the full-length mirror to the right of the room's door.

He stands in front of the table and looks out the window down at the Frontier Room and Cigarette. The green and orange neon of the Frontier Room's sign and the white-with-a-red-tip neon cigarette that is Cigarette's only sign. Little knots of people scurrying the few steps through the rain from one place to the other. Mary's tired but restless.

He looks down at the two bars he's spent so many years in.

If he goes over there right now no one will be saying anything they hadn't been saying earlier this afternoon when he was last there, or were saying last night for that matter. Maybe some new gossip will be circulating. But its quality and importance will be doubtful. As always, as usual, as ever, it'll be the same assortment of failed prospects assembled in the standard postures and cliques.

Besides, it's kind of nice to have the place to himself. And if there's anything really worth hearing about he'll get it from Sayyid Husayn when he comes back to their room.

Mary decides to just stay home. He goes around the room plugging in and turning on the various colored lights. The three lava lamps on the windowsill above the table, multiple strings of miniature flashing Christmas lights, the little statues, figurines and souvenirs which are internally or externally illuminated. Mary sheds his pumps, turns off the overhead lights and opens the radiator all the way. It immediately starts hissing and gurgling as it fills with hot water. He sits in the one really comfortable chair in the place and watches the lava lamps warm up. Two red ones with a blue one in between them.

Twenty minutes later the storm that's been hovering over Seattle all evening picks up again. Rattling and splattering the windows. A "quality" storm is really quite enough reason in itself to stay home with the festive party lights and enjoy its passing.

Mary gets out of his skirt, slip and stockings and sits on the bed. Pillows stacked behind him and blankets pulled over his legs, up to his waist. He puffs a couple times on a fresh cigarette then digs a cassette of The Fall out of the pile next to him and puts it in the box. A minute later he leans back over and turns up the volume to help drown out "The Price Is Right" blasting on a TV in the room below.

Once the radiator is blazing Mary gets up and goes back to the table, picks up a small metal box and takes out the little pipe and a piece of hashish wrapped in cellophane. He takes a hit or two and watches people across the street coming and going. The Fall ends and now the canned laughter from "Cheers" is pulsating up into the room. He puts in a cassette of Sonic Youth's "Sister" album and turns it up several notches.

Now sitting at the table Mary sees a figure down in front of Cigarette with a red rain slicker held over their head. This is most likely Edith. The two people with him look to be Ruby and Murrow. Just seeing these familiars going about The Routine satisfies all desires Mary has to be there with them.

The Frontier Room and Cigarette as his Living Room and Rec Room.

Mary thinks of all those nights and all that gin. He smiles picturing an Olympic-size pool with Tanqueray and Bombay lapping at the edges.

To walk back and forth. Stroll, sit down, eat, drink, chat, look around; TV flashing, jukebox pumping. But not tonight.

22

SPOKANE–MISSOULA

And there were pilgrimages. The most profound of which were to Missoula, Montana.

In the mid-1960s a pious and wealthy Missoula benefactor purchased a hill on the northern edge of the city. She spent a large sum of money having the summit of the hill cleared and leveled. Cutting off the top of it so that it looked more like a mesa than anything you find around that part of the country. A narrow switchback was carved out and paved from the base to the top.

A few months later a caravan of trucks crawled their way up the narrow road. Over the next several days a crew of workers assembled a four-story-high icon of Mary, Mother of God, Queen of Angels. Created of cement, plywood, plexiglass, fiberglass and many, many gallons of paint. The statue was encircled with small but powerful spotlights. And finally, one summer night, the pious patron flipped the switch and the hilltop was engulfed in light. Our Lady bright, luminous and vigilant over the city.

The road up the hill leads to a circular drive around the icon so that She can be appreciated intimately from all angles. As you drive by the front of the statue you pass a brass plaque explaining who paid for Her and when She was installed.

Between Her and the spotlights is a broad strip of well-kept grass. A tall chainlink fence circumscribes the spots. At night the hilltop is flooded with harsh white light and up close She is very coarse in design and appearance. But from a distance She is a glowing mysterious apparition.

For reasons the benefactor took with her to the grave she had this vast icon fashioned in the image of Our Lady of the Sorrows.

Our Lady is very much a commonplace for Missoula's residents and the frequent travelers to and through the city. But to Sheila The Lady on the hill is a sight so sacred and cathartic that the merest thought or mention of it sends her into a very physical rapture.

The first time Sheila saw Her was as a kid traveling with her parents to an uncle's ranch in southeast Montana. Sheila begged and whined and pleaded until she started getting a nosebleed and her parents finally agreed to stop in Missoula to see Her on their way home to Spokane.

On long weekends and in the long hot summer the six of them find a car (usually Harvey's) and take trips. They alternate between Seattle and Missoula. After the first few pilgrimages to Missoula there is talk of moving there. Once they've created the basement grotto they make a special trip to Missoula and return with a bucket full of dirt from near the icon's feet and several Polaroids of Her. They sprinkle some of the dirt around their own small icon and store the rest in coffee cans.

This particular pilgrimage is in the last week of June. They'd started the day by eating handfuls of crisscross speed. They pile into Harvey's late '60s four-door Oldsmobile sedan and drive around and around Spokane. Drinking beer, smoking marijuana and grinding their teeth. By early afternoon they've gone everywhere and done everything there is to do in Spokane.

It's right around 2 pm. They're idling at a stoplight. Sheila is counting the remaining tablets of speed in the small baby food jar. Tabulation complete she stares out the window thinking. She sits up straight and is now very excited. Harvey glances over at her. That look on her face is enough to tell him where she wants to go. He looks at the needle showing a little under half a tank of gasoline and tries to remember how much money he has on him. Sheila shakes the jar of crisscrosses like a rattle and says:

"Alright! Let's go to Missoula! We've got enough of these to last us through tomorrow. Let's go visit The Lady."

Douglas jumps forward and leans over the seat with a big smile on his face.

"Yeah! Excellent! If we stop by my house I can get some more money and we can get some more beer!"

"We gotta get some more tapes. I'm tired of these."

The plan gets stalled for a while by Douglas' dad. The old man is drunk (of course) and is in one of his contrary and suspicious moods. Usually, even though he is the youngest devotee (14), Douglas has the easiest time staying away from home whenever and however long he wants to because his dad is so wrapped up in his vodka and girlfriends. But today the booze is having an embittering effect. Despite his father's screams they finally just leave. Douglas' dad is too drunk to get off the couch and do anything about it.

Another half-rack of Rainier and some different cassettes and they hit eastbound Interstate 90.

The closer they get to Missoula the more hyped and twitchy Sheila gets and the louder she turns up the car stereo. They'd listened to Roxy Music and David Bowie and then Sheila puts in a "best of" Led Zeppelin cassette. When it's finished she convinces them to let her play it again, even louder. Then again, and again.

It's five o'clock or so when they exit the freeway into Missoula. Sheila leans out the car window and looks right up at Her. But after a second she retracts her body and averts her eyes. Sheila does not consider it proper to gaze upon Her in the drab and unflattering light of day.

Sheila's jaws are really starting to ache, and Harriet's complaining that the glaring sun is painfully harsh on her eyes.

"Okay. Let's go see if we can get a room in the Rocky Mountain."

Five of the six pilgrimages to see Her they stay at the Rocky Mountain View Motel. The last couple of times they've shown up in her office wanting rooms the woman who owns and manages the Rocky Mountain View stopped squinting hostilely over her reading glasses at them. They've never damaged any of the rooms and there's never been any complaints from other guests about their behavior. And they always pay in cash.

The first time they chose the Rocky Mountain View Motel

because from the motel's parkinglot there is an excellent view of Her. Right there in the middle of the northern skyline, bright and hovering on the hill. Her arms are raised, bent at the elbows, hands at waist level, palms open and facing up. A gesture of sadness and empathy. A recognition of having nothing to really soothe or ease the suffering, except Her empathy.

Harriet and Douglas stay in the room while the rest of them spend the early evening in and around the motel's pool. Harriet is not feeling so well; too much speed. Douglas is afraid of drowning and generally doesn't like water. The two of them are curled up together on a bed. The shades are drawn. The room is dark and cool and the hum of the AC masks any outdoor sounds.

The sun heads down west and out of sight. Swimming for several hours has worn down the amphetamine energy. They all shower and all eat more speed.

And now is the time for prayer in preparation for the trip up the hill. And these prayers before they go see Her are performed naked except for their rosaries and strings of religious trinkets and medals around their necks. Douglas and Raeann think this aspect of their cult is very cool and exciting. All that nudity. To them it is very exotic and erotic and involves a level of trust (which they perceive as bonding) that seems very religious. Harvey likes it because it lets him visually devour the others' nakedness. Harriet and Fred find it somewhat uncomfortable. Harriet because Harvey stares at her so incessantly. Fred finds it difficult because he is so attracted to Harvey and Harvey never looks at him anything like the way he does the girls.

Sheila preaches that their bodies are the only physical gift given to each soul to help ease the separation from the Divine. Nakedness of the body while praying, and the pleasures experienced with it, function as expressions of gratitude to the Mother of God for bestowing their displaced souls with something to pass the time with, and perhaps, for a moment, forget the troubles of life.

At this point in time the varieties of erotic bonding between them are not yet acted upon. Sheila has had the word that there's to be no fucking each other yet. Sheila has it all planned out. In a few weeks perhaps.

For now when the prayers are done they all get dressed. Sheila distributes more crisscrosses, two on every tongue. In a short time everyone is buzzing and restless. By now it is fully nighttime.

Sheila yanks open the room's door and runs out into the middle of the motel's parkinglot. She raises her arms with a flourish and does a slight bow of greeting to her Friend on the hill. The Lady is sort of shivering, shimmering, but still She smiles. That half-sad, half-puzzled smile. Sheila slumps to her knees, swaying from side to side muttering the Rosary. Douglas runs out of the room, stopping a few feet behind her. He looks up. He crouches and starts feverishly reciting the Rosary, trying to catch up with Sheila so they can be in synch. Four adults leaving the motel's coffee shop stop and stare at the two teenagers on their knees in the parkinglot.

Harvey steps out of the AC-chilled room into the still and hot night. He smiles at his two friends. Then he sees the adults staring, his grin fades. Quickly but quietly he walks up behind Douglas.

"Doug. Doug. Come on guy. You gotta get up. There's people staring..."

The youngest angel looks up at his friend (Doug's green eyes glowing), glances over at the adults, then back at Harvey.

"I don't give a fuck about... those..."

"I know, I just don't want nothin' to stop us from going up to see Her..."

Harvey gestures up at the icon with his brown eyes. Douglas follows his glance and his eyes lock onto The Lady. He nods slightly and starts to stand up.

"Yeah. Yeah, you're right. Okay. I'm ready..."

Now Raeann and Harriet are standing with the two boys. Harriet says:

"I'll get Doug in the car. You two get Sheila."

Gently gripping Douglas' arm Harriet leads him over to the car where Fred is already settled into the back seat. Raeann and Harvey crouch down on either side of Sheila.

"Hey girl, time to go... She's waiting..."

Sheila murmurs the end of a Hail Mary and then smiles at her friends. She stands and stuffs her rosary into one of her jeans' pockets as they walk over to the Oldsmobile. Her hands are dripping sweat; she tries to dry them on her T-shirt.

23

"Turn it up, turn it up!"

Fred leans over the front seat, grabs the volume and jerks it to the right. Jimi Hendrix jumps and his guitar shrieks all the louder.

Even Harvey is starting to let go and get over worrying about them getting intercepted by the police or some other adult power. What the fuck, they're almost to the top of the hill. As long as there's nobody else up there already everything is groovy.

The Queen of Heaven is visible now from the waist up. Harvey thumps the accelerator down and the car shoots around the last twists of the road, back and forth, left right left right, screech screech. They fly over a speed bump, the front bumper scrapes the pavement shooting sparks, they careen around a third of the circular drive and then Harvey stomps on the brakes. The tires shred against the pavement and the stink of heated rubber drifts around the sedan and up into the darkness.

Sheila punches off the stereo and jerks the passenger door open. Harvey gets out, goes to the back of the car and opens the trunk. He takes out a pair of heavy-duty wire cutters and a pair of thick work gloves.

Snip, snip. Snip, snip, snip. Harvey cuts diagonally from the ground to about three and a half feet up in the links of the fence that circles the icon. Fred puts the cutters away and closes the trunk. Harvey, gloves still on, pulls at the cut section of fence creating a triangular opening. Sheila slips in first. A few paces inside, just beyond the ring of spotlights, she gets down on her belly and commences crawling. She is straining her neck back to keep Her face always in sight. Sheila scrambles forward using knees and elbows. After the rest are through Harvey brings up the rear. Raeann holds the fence open from the inside. Harvey crawls through, butt jutting up, waggling about.

At the base near Her feet they all stop. Sitting on knees each begins their own personalized liturgy. One by one they kiss Her concrete feet.

Time passes and Douglas is praying so hard he starts getting the sweating and nausea that comes on him when he goes into religious overdrive. Fred is feeling a little ill too. Harvey is sitting right next to him. Harvey's left arm, big-muscled and bare below his T-shirt sleeve, is warm and electric against his own arm. Fred looks at Harvey from the corner of his eye. He sees Harvey looking at Sheila and Raeann. Fred knows that Harvey wants to fuck both of them. Fred is a little sick to his stomach because he is pretty sure Harvey does not consider him in the same way he does the girls. Maybe Sheila can make it alright.

Suddenly it feels like a finger is poking into Fred's mind. He looks up. Her elbows are bent, arms outstretched at waist level. Hands open, palms up. She watches, She beckons. She is looking out over the whole city and the whole world and at him. Fred wants to cry with frustration. She pats him on the shoulder. Fred glances back at Harvey's face. The brilliant, nearly blinding light from the spots reflecting off the icon washes Harvey's face out to dead white. Fred's throat constricts. He closes his eyes and he can feel the thudding of his own heart.

Nearly two hours go by. Everyone has finished their rituals and ceremonies.

Harriet (who doesn't usually smoke) bums a Marlboro from Fred. She inhales deeply several times until the nicotine hits her system like the world is pushing in on her from all sides. Without a word she hands the half-smoked cigarette to Douglas, then flops onto her back on the grass staring up at the stars. The world swirls and pushes.

Harvey is rolling a joint. He licks the gummed edge. Sheila is watching his progress. She says:

"I think we oughta start bringing special stuff to leave for Her. Gifts, presents. We should leave something for Her tonight... I wish to fuck I'd thought of this back home..."

Raeann exhales a lung full of marijuana smoke and jumps to her feet.

"Hey, shit! I got it!"

Raeann runs back to the fence, out and over to the car. She leans in the driver's side window until her feet are a couple of inches off the asphalt. She returns with something cupped in her hands. She stands with her arms outstretched then slowly opens her hands so her friends sitting on the grass can see what she has. It is her Led Zeppelin cassette they'd listened to for most of the trip over from Spokane. Sheila's face softens with awe and relief. She looks up at Raeann. Raeann hands her the cassette with all due ceremony. Raeann stands there all smiles, hands jammed down into her faded Levis' pockets.

"Yeah... this is it... you sure you want to leave it here?"

"Shit yes! You fucking bet! What else do we got that's good enough?"

Raeann is almost indignant.

"Okay, I was just makin' sure."

"I think we should bury it around here."

"What if we... cut a secret hole in the... uh... base thing, and each time we come we'll hide somethin' new in it..."

"Yeah right, how are we gonna cut through concrete?"

"No, I think burying things is the best idea."

"Yeah, every time we come we'll dig another hole. Until there's stuff all the way around Her!"

"Too bad we don't have a picture of all of us to bury with the tape..."

"Yeah..."

They settle on burying the Zeppelin cassette in front of Her right foot. Screwdrivers are used to gouge out a small section of the grass, then loosen up the dirt beneath so a hole can be scooped out by hand. They very carefully tamp the dirt back in and replace the swatch of turf.

Over the next year or so of pilgrimages they leave nearly 20 offerings. Buried in little holes in a clockwise circle around Her base.

And there are photos of them offered up. Group portraits, individual poses. And then when Sheila finally does orchestrate the sex thing there is a stack of two dozen Polaroids fastened with a red rubberband buried near the left heel of the Mother of God.

24

SEATTLE

On a whim (or at the lure of evil djinn) Mary decides they should chance it and rove outside of Belltown. They are gonna go up to Capitol Hill. Capitol Hill had been a fine place before Money moved in. Now it is just a hunting ground. They walk up Pike Street and pause in a few of the upscale homosexual bars on the way. Nothing and no one. They end up in Ernie Steele's which had been the best cocktail lounge on the Hill. They only manage two drinks apiece before they're in an argument and then a bit of shoving with three suits and their dates and end up 86'd.

They head back downtown on Union Street because it is less traveled and because it passes through First Hill. First Hill is the neighborhood just south of Capitol Hill where Mary had lived years ago. He points out his old building and they creep around peering in windows to see if it looks the same on the inside. It doesn't.

First Hill is all hospitals and renovated red brick apartment buildings. Nice and quiet so they stroll and chat. Zigzag along residential streets and alleys.

As they turn onto a street they hear screams from somewhere nearby. Approaching an alley the screams are louder and Mary and Sayyid Husayn can hear vicious male voices yelling and cursing.

Now, neither Mary nor Sayyid Husayn are do-gooders by any means. But they've always liked a good fight and sticking their noses in other people's trouble, if they are in the mood.

At the alley entrance they pause, listen, and slowly move in, keeping close to the buildings.

Near the other end of the alley there are five or six men in a semicircle around another man who is crouched down, back to the brick wall, arms up and over his face trying to protect it. Sayyid Husayn lightly touches Mary's shoulder and they halt their advance. The shouts of abuse are very clear now.

"Faggot!"

"You wanna suck my dick faggot?! Come on cocksucker answer me!"

"You want us to fuck you with this piece of pipe faggot?! It's nice and big. Huh. Yeah... fucking queer..."

Each curse is punctuated with kicks and punches.

Mary's got nothing against criminals doing their jobs, but he hates stupidity. It's one thing to molest people because of who they've chosen to be or the class they are striving to exemplify, but pounding on someone because of their color or who they like to fuck bugs the shit out of Mary. Fagbashers are the lowest. Fucking cowards never go after someone on their own, always gotta have the other guys along. Pathetic cowards. Suckie little bastards. Better off dead.

Mary reaches for his revolver and Sayyid Husayn does the same. Mary whispers:

"Go back around the block to the other end of the alley. I'll do a slow count to 50 and then move in."

Sayyid Husayn scampers off, Mary starts rubbing his thumb on the butt of his revolver and slowly counting.

"... 47... 48... 49... and... 50..."

Clutching the revolver inside his parka pocket Mary pushes off the safety and stalks down the alley. Scrape, scrape go his heels on the paving bricks.

"Alright! Back off! Do you shits hear me! Back off! Leave him alone!"

The men halt their actions in mid-curse and swing. They assume it's the police. But it is quickly apparent Mary is not the police. One of them laughs. Mary's eyes shift back and forth, waiting for one of them to become the target. A couple of them laugh and this tall burly guy steps forward and raises the length of steel pipe he's been threatening the man crouched in front of him with.

"Yeah? Who the fuck are you! Another faggot! In fucking high heels! Jesusfuckingchrist! Listen faggot you better get the fuck out of here! Maybe I'll just cut you a real pussy like you want! Huh, whaddaya say about that faggot?!"

Mary's kept his handgun in his coat pocket up to now. He stands, not really listening to what the man says, he is planning his shot. Mary smiles a little. The man with the pipe starts to move menacingly toward him. The man spits laughter and glances back at his buddies to make sure they're catching all this.

Mary lifts the revolver, grips the butt with both hands and shoots the man in the head, right above and in front of the left ear. As the shithead drops dead to the pavement one of the other men screams and they turn trying to escape. But Sayyid Husayn is there, his weapon is raised and cocked. Trapped, the group of men freeze, drop their weapons and raise their hands. One of them says hoarsely:

"Hey man... don't shoot... we'll give you our money... just relax man..."

Mary is relaxed and warm with pleasure. He smiles.

"Oh, now he says, 'don't shoot.' Well, isn't that nice. Alright, you and your buttbuddies get up against the wall over there..."

He gestures to the brick wall opposite the victim. While Mary keeps an eye on the bashers Sayyid Husayn checks the target of the attack. A few bruises and scrapes but nothing much. The man remains cowering, shivering and sobbing. Sayyid Husayn stands up.

"Yeah, he's alright..."

Sayyid Husayn goes over to their prisoners and gives them a thorough patting down. He gropes their crotches, squeezing their testicles until they wince. None of them dare complain. Sayyid Husayn collects what money they have and a watch that looks like it might be worth something.

"Very nice boys, very nice. Now, take off your pants, all of you. Underwear too."

"Hey man, what you want us to do that for? Come on man, you got the money, just let us go..."

Mary lurches forward and shoves the barrel of his .38 into the man's throat just below his chin. Mary's eyes are wide and unblinking.

"You, you could die right now. *Right now*..."

The man turns an ugly greenish. His whine goes to a whimper.

"*Hey!... Please...*"

" *'Please'* ?! You wanna beg *me* for *your* life?... It's a little fucking late for that... *honey*..."

Mary steps back and points the revolver at their victim hunched down against the wall. No longer crying, just watching very closely everything that happens.

"Didn't do this dumbshit much good, now did it. *'Please, please.'* No. No pleasing me fuckface! Not you..."

"Mary! Mary listen..."

Sayyid Husayn cuts in on his boyfriend's spitting hiss. Mary stops and takes a deep breath. Sirens are moving nearer from the east.

"Alright! I know!"

He turns back to the line of men.

"Get your fucking pants off now! All of you! Now! And your panties too kids!"

Without further words shoes and pants and underwear are taken off. They stand close together looking scared. Mary makes a brief show of scrutinizing their penises and asses and making disparaging remarks about their poor examples of manhood.

"Now listen closely boys! I want you all to remember one thing.... *We* rule the streets... *we* do..."

He waves the barrel of his .38 in a single all-encompassing gesture.

"If I ever see, or hear, of any of you again, you are dead. Dead. Understand? Good.

"Now get the fuck outta of my sight! Go. No! Leave your clothes right there..."

The bugs scuttle away, nearly falling over each other. Mary and Sayyid Husayn are laughing so hard they are coughing. The victim looks from them to the dead man lying on the bricks with a large section of his skull and brain missing. He starts to stand up using the wall to steady himself.

"Jesus..."

Mary turns and looks at him. Hysteria flickers across the man's face from moment to moment. He keeps staring at the dead man. Mary's lips twitch into a brief sneer.

"Yeah, well... they were gonna do you up good, buddy. Real good... better him than you huh?"

"I... I guess... shit... I'm bleeding... my leg..."

He grips his upper right thigh. Sayyid Husayn leans down and squints at the patch of blood and torn denim. He straightens up and shrugs deprecatingly.

"A few stitches..."

Mary is giving him a look-over, beyond just his wounds and traumas. Two gold chains around his neck, a gold Rolex on his left wrist, a gold bracelet on his other, and gold ear- and finger rings.

"Okay, honey. You'll be just fine. We saved your worthless hide. So give us all that gold you're wearing. All of it."

"What?! You... you two, saved my life... why do you wanna rob me? Please, after what they did to me?! Please..."

"Shut-the-fuck-up. I don't give a shit about *you*. It's them, those shits that motivated me to step in. It's them I hate. I don't give a shit about you. Your kind wouldn't give me the time of day if we were on your turf. You're obviously a stupid vulgar asshole who doesn't know any fucking better than to get lured into an alley by a bunch of fagbashers! Now hurry up, those sirens are getting close."

The man is shaking badly but manages to be fast about turning over the goods.

"Please... my ID..."

"Yeah, yeah. What do I want with it, or these keys..."

Mary plucks cash and plastic out of the expensive lambskin wallet and hands the wallet and a ring of keys back. The man had been carrying a good wad of bills.

"And another thing dumbfuck. *Never* carry this much cash if you're going out cruising. What, are you really as stupid as you look?"

The sirens are much closer now.

"Okay dear, just sit tight and help'll be here soon. We gotta go... be more careful..."

Mary and Sayyid Husayn run, run, run all the way home.

A half an hour or so later and the two of them are back in their room counting the cash ($448.63). Mary says:

"There's another part of the city I never fucking wanna see again."

Sayyid Husayn shrugs as he uses his folding knife to shave off bits from the block of hashish into the little pipe.

25

MARY

Inside his head, in his dead-of-night dreams, a tiny mournful voice from a distant minaret is calling the faithful to prayer.

I remember one time. It was late at night. I'd gotten off work at De Ville's about an hour earlier. I was curled up under the blankets with Husayn. He was already undressed and in bed before I got home. He is sleeping soundly. I'd shed my pumps, stockings and skirt. I'm warming up and listening to the wind and the sparse traffic of this hour of the night down on 1st Avenue.

I start thinking of getting up and smoking a cigarette, but it's so damn cold. The fucking steam heat is already off for the night. But I still have to take off my makeup and wash so I brace myself to get out into it. Whatever.

Husayn starts twitching. I can see his lips and tongue moving soundlessly. Without seeming to wake he rises up onto his elbows and looks at the small alarm clock on the floor on my side of the bed. He crawls out of my semi-embrace and off the bed on all fours, dragging himself to the eastern wall of our room.

There between the dresser and door, down about waist-level, he has pinned up a tattered black-and-white snapshot of an elderly Arabic woman. At first I'd thought this must be his mother or something like that. He'd scowled and curtly informed me that this woman, as the blessed Elder, is the living online uplink with the Household of the Messenger Muhammad (pbut). On the floor beneath this photo is a well-worn paperback copy of the Quran in Arabic that he keeps wrapped in a piece of black cotton cloth and propped against the wall.

Husayn gets to his feet and in motions smooth with innumerable repetitions begins to pray.

First, if he has not actually washed with water, gestures

of ritual cleansing; palms wiping lower legs, forearms, head and then face. Next the arms raised to the heavens followed by the verbal intro. More prescribed gestures and verbal formulas with appropriate prostrations and postures. And depending on which of the Quranicly mandated daily prayers it is (and personal desires), a sura or two.

Not that I understand a word of Arabic, but he's explained it all.

Husayn's never tried any evangelizing with me. Or anyone else that I know of. His faith has nothing to do with anybody else. It's just him and The One Divine.

I lay still and watch.

His forehead briefly and lightly touches the floor; one cycle of the prayer is ending. I close my eyes and listen to the soft melodic roll of his half-whispered Arabic.

The ritualized cleansing thing really used to bother me. I mean especially after he explained that it is particularly important if he is praying shortly after we've been fucking. This really pissed me off for quite a while. I mean, what isn't good enough about me that he can't go before God smelling of? But as I got to know him it became obvious that what he and his deity have going does not really have anything to do with me.

It's nothing personal, him needing to be at least symbolically clean after fucking. It's just that Husayn's One Divine is not so much monotheistic as monogamous. I get the picture. Boys are like that. Or not. Whatever. Keep one situation separate from the other. Or not.

As if God is right there; greedy eyes and all-knowing. Husayn on his knees, spindly legs rocking back and forth as he grips my waist. Twitch. Twitch. The Ninety-Nine Names on his lips as he orgasms in blindness.

Sayyid Husayn — he is *very* big on making sure people know he has "Sayyid" at the beginning of his name because it signifies that he is a genetic descendant of the Household of the Messenger (pbut) through the Messenger's daughter Fatima (peace be upon her). Not that anyone around here has any clear idea of what that all means...

Anyway, Husayn loves God, a lot.

It helps him shoot straight and keeps him calmer than he might otherwise be. So I don't mind anymore. Husayn seems perfectly capable of keeping both of us happy.

26

Mary never wonders what he believes in or does not believe in. This lack of doubt, this resignation, is how he survives and prospers.

Mary does not worry that Sayyid Husayn will someday no longer love him. Or might "desert" him. He does not worry about this because he does not "believe" Sayyid Husayn "loves" him. That would be like believing or not believing in the existence of air or water. It is not something he spends any time on.

And Sayyid Husayn? Sayyid Husayn does not "believe" either. He has an organic faith in everything to do with Mary. Sayyid Husayn is all faith. To be alive from one hour to the next is acting in faith to Sayyid Husayn. *Incha Allah.* "If God wills it."

Sayyid Husayn's faith is nothing cheap and smelling of sweaty nylon and aftershave like some Bible-thumper or something.

27

From where they sit the clock over the bar is just a glowing white disk with black slashes on its face.

Edith is the only one who hasn't finished his drink yet. He keeps going on and on about having finally gotten a boyfriend. Mary looks at Ruby, she looks over at the clock and then back at Mary. Mary interrupts Edith's raving happiness.

"Alright. Anthony Carlton is a divine entity. So let's get a move on and get to the speak-easy before all the decent gin is gone."

Edith lurches forward drunkenly, leans across the table and pats Mary on the cheek. He tilts his head to one side and sneers.

"You are *so* fucking sweet. Just because *you've* been getting it regular forever is no reason to lose your compassion for the less fortunate among us."

That said he slurps down the rest of his cocktail, grabs his purse and coat and staggers to his feet. The others all turn to leave but Edith heads to the payphone in back instead.

"Anthony wants me to call him before we leave so he can meet me there..."

"We're thrilled for you..."

Mary and Ruby are the first ones outside. Ruby leans against the wall smoking and humming to some song by My Dad Is Dead that has been running in her head all evening. Wind picks up some trash off of 1st Avenue, scattering and rearranging it a few feet farther down the street. Above them, chunks of clouds careen past the bright half-moon. The moon's white light flashes on and off.

10 minutes later the seven of them trudge up Bell Street from 1st Avenue to the alley between 1st and 2nd and head north.

John, Jane and Edith go dashing ahead. Frantic drunken hollering. Screeched snatches of songs interrupting each other, pulling and pushing incoherent.

Edith falls down. He rolls back and forth waving his legs in the air shrieking that he can't take another step without his man. The other two pick him up and try to brush the grit off his coat. They stumble on a few more steps. John trips and hits the ground. Edith and Jane cough and gasp in hysterics. On their feet again they hurl themselves down the alley. Each belting out a competing tune.

Ruby, Murrow, Mary and Sayyid Husayn are a little less than half a dozen yards behind. Floating on their alcohol buzz, conversations digressing all over the place.

About a block from the speak-easy the three in the

vanguard pass next to a large parkinglot situated between 1st and the alley. The lot is almost empty. On the edge of the lot near the alley a dark-colored Camaro is parked. The passenger door is open and Guns N' Roses is pounding out one of their monotonous tunes on the car stereo. When Edith, Jane and John are about a third of the way past the parkinglot a young man jumps from the car and strides rapidly toward them.

"Hey Edith! What's up? C'mere."

The three stop, still laughing at some joke. Edith squints and then recognizes the man as his very own Anthony Carlton.

"Baby! Honey! Loverboy! What are you doin' here? I thought you were gonna meet me at the speak-easy?!..."

Edith waves his arms about and stumbles toward Carlton. As Edith gets close two more men pile out of the car. They are both clutching Mac-10s close to their chests. They are looking for a man in a dress and the first thing they see when they get out of the Camaro is a man in a skirt talking to Carlton. Anthony Carlton, meanwhile, is looking past Edith, Jane and John, up the alley in the direction they'd come. In a worried whisper he says:

"Edith where's Mary?"

"Mary?!"

Edith is slightly disoriented because Anthony won't embrace him and irritated because his supposed boyfriend is asking for his cousin. Behind Anthony Carlton the gunmen scoot a little closer and snap back the levers on their machineguns. When Carlton hears this very particular sound he goes very pale. He turns back toward the car and sees the shooters are ready. He tries desperately to discreetly shake his head no. He is suddenly scared and jerks away from Edith's grasp. In the second before the assassins open fire Carlton realizes two things. That the gunmen have mistaken this transvestite for the one they have been sent to kill, and that they have been instructed to kill him along with their primary target.

Mary and Ruby have just reached the corner of the building that abuts the southeast corner of the parkinglot. They'd stopped talking when they heard the man call out to Edith. As they step into full view of the parkinglot they see Carlton and Edith, and Jane and John a few feet beyond them. And they see the two men standing by the Camaro with "street sweepers" at ready. It is not instantly apparent who or what they are except trouble. Sirens go off in Mary and Ruby's minds and firearms are reached for. Mary manages to yell one word before things happen.

"Edith!..."

Anthony Carlton is pointing at Mary and shrieking (as he pisses his pants with fear).

"No, No! It's *him*..."

This is when the shooting starts. The shooters spray Edith, his supposed boyfriend, John and Jane.

Edith and Carlton are immediately dead. John falls to the asphalt screaming, clutching his guts and kicking his heels on the pavement. Crouching next to her dying husband Jane draws her Glock 9mm automatic. There is blood on her left arm and shoulder. Is it from John or from herself? She manages one shot before another burst splatters her with lead.

The shooters have not seen the four bringing up the rear. They saw a man in a skirt and started firing.

Sayyid Husayn drops and rolls several feet and ends prone, pistol drawn. He shoots one of the gunmen in the chest. Ruby is leaning forward around the corner of the building, gripping her Ingram and snapping off bursts. Her mouth open in wordless fury. Murrow is kneeling beside her, ready for an attack from behind. Ruby's fire gives Mary the cover to dash over to Edith's body. Gunshots and ricochets reverberate and there is screaming.

Very shortly it is all over. The gunfire ends but Guns N' Roses pounds on. The assassins are both on the ground near the car; one is moaning and trying to pull himself into the Camaro. Mary is kneeling next to Edith. Murrow and Ruby go to the Camaro. The wounded man turns and looks up at them. Murrow kicks him in the face and then shoots him twice. He is silent. They kick the other man several times as hard as they can to make sure he is dead. Ruby steps over them, leans into the car and shuts off the music. She yanks out the cassette and hurls it into the parkinglot. Ruby is standing with one pump's heel in a pool of blood, scanning for any more trouble. Murrow is crouched down checking out the hitmen. She taps Ruby's leg. Ruby looks down and Murrow is gripping one of the men's wrists. On the ring finger he is wearing a silver band of small skulls. This is the badge of membership in the Fiances of Death. A quick check determines the other is wearing the same ring.

Mary is resting crouched on the balls of his feet, revolver clutched tightly, staring at the bloody carnage that was Edith's chest. He softly touches his cousin's face, running a finger lightly along the cheekbone. Edith's mouth is ajar and his eyes full of surprise. Mary closes the eyelids. From each of Edith's ears Mary removes the earrings Edith was wearing that night. They had been Edith's favorite pair.

Sayyid Husayn is standing nearby, eyes scanning for any more Fiances who may be lurking. Mary looks up and around.

"Husayn, his purse... I think it's over there. I don't want it to go to scavengers..."

Sayyid Husayn starts to say something but doesn't. The red vinyl outsize handbag is several feet beyond where Edith lies.

Mary suddenly jumps up. He looks back and forth from Edith's corpse to Carlton's. Mary kicks Anthony Carlton's body as hard as he can, over and over.

"Fuck you... traitor... you fucking used him! It was me wasn't it?! It was me you were s'posed to get!..."

"*Mary!* Mary."

Ruby snaps his name out like an order. She walks over to him, almost cautious like she's not sure what he might do next. Ruby reaches over slowly and slides one arm around his waist and in a quieter voice says:

"We gotta go... we gotta get outta here honey... they're all... dead, honey... we gotta go. Now."

She turns to Murrow who is standing back in the alley keeping an eye out for more of the opposition.

"Find the keys to John and Jane's room; we'll go there... Husayn, c'mere and help me with him..."

Sayyid Husayn goes to his boyfriend's side and replaces Ruby's arm around Mary's waist. He doesn't say anything, just moves up close to Mary. He can feel Mary shivering slightly.

The hollow-point ammunition the Fiances were using made it unnecessary to check their friends for vital signs. With a minimum of rummaging Murrow locates John's set of keys.

Only Sayyid Husayn looks back at the parkinglot as the survivors scuttle away. He recites a short prayer for the dead as he takes up the rear guard.

28

Down other alleys, cautiously along sidewalks, they weave their way to the Savoy Hotel were John and Jane lived. Ruby picked their place because it might be safer since it is not in Belltown. John and Jane had refused to leave the hotel and move to Belltown with the rest of the crew.

Ruby goes in the front and through the lobby trying to be casual. No one notices a bit of dry blood on the heel of her left pump. The others wait in the alley behind the hotel. A couple of minutes and Ruby is letting them in the rear door. To avoid the Savoy's other residents they work their way up the back stairs to John and Jane's room.

Once they're in the room no one moves to turn on any lights. Murrow is near the windows keeping an eye on 2nd Avenue below. Ruby is pacing back and forth. She looks at Mary hoping he'll come back into reality and help her, but no. Sayyid Husayn and Mary are on the small couch near the TV. Sayyid Husayn's left hand is at Mary's neck slowly and gently massaging it. Mary is unmoving. He hasn't said a word since they left the scene of the massacre. He is slumped down, nearly lifeless, his head drooping forward. Twisted with guilt and failure. For so many years he'd been his younger cousin's protector and mentor. And now Edith was killed because he was mistaken for Mary. Killed because of something Mary'd done and had been so sure he could keep a handle on. Mary feels fear. The fear has nothing to do with Fiances wanting to kill him, Mary is scared because he had calculated so badly and because he is not in control of the world around him. He has failed the posse, three of the Straight Shooters' best are dead because of his miscalculation. Sayyid Husayn gets up and goes to where Jane kept her gun-cleaning stuff. Back on the couch he sets to work on his and Mary's revolvers.

Ruby stops in front of the couch.

"Carlton was just, uh... his thing with Edith was... we saw their rings... you know... they were... Fiances... .They were using Edith to find you..."

Mary doesn't look up or respond. Ruby knows Mary has probably figured out who they were and why the assassins were there waiting for them. Ruby wishes Mary would just look at her and say something, anything to show he is still there to fight at her side. Even punch her in the face for being so mean to him.

"Edith was just in the line of fire... probably looking for a guy in a dress... and they saw him first..."

Ruby starts to say more but doesn't. She feels a cold distance between herself and Mary that has never been there in all their years. All their years. Ruby turns away and goes to the phone and makes several calls.

Ruby walks over to her purse and rummages for her cigarettes. Not finding them she grimaces with frustration and then thinks to check the pockets of her car coat which she has not taken off. Finding the Marlboros she stuffs the filter-tip between her lips. A further search of pockets produces no matches or lighter. She walks over to her girlfriend who lights the cigarette. She speaks in a tense low whisper.

"A bomb... a bomb in Cigarette.... That was Bontemp, he was sitting at the window of his place and then there was a loud blast and a second later a flash of fire a couple blocks away... by the time he got there most of the block was in flames... he was calling from a phone booth at 3rd and Bell..."

"Murrow, stick your head out and look in that direction... can you see anything?"

"Uh, maybe... I can't tell for sure..."

Ruby starts to say more. How many dead? How many Straight Shooters were in Cigarette and the Frontier Room? She takes a long drag on the Marlboro instead. Murrow leans forward and touches her girlfriend's face. Ruby looks at her and then walks back to the phone.

"I gotta find Eagle Chief..."

Sayyid Husayn finishes with the pistols. After reloading them he puts his in his holster and the other in Mary's purse. Sayyid Husayn is waiting. Waiting for Mary. Waiting for Ruby to give orders.

Ruby finishes her phone calls. Nothing and no one gives her guidance, just catastrophe and facts. Ruby wishes she had gotten out of being the boss a long time ago. Too late now.

Murrow leaves the window and moves to her girl-friend's side.

"We *gotta* hit back Ruby. Not just for the posse's morale... if we're not out there tonight hitting back, hard... then there's not gonna be nothing left... we slide and every fucking prick in the county and their fucking pubescent brothers are gonna come stomping in here and rip it to pieces..."

Ruby looks at her half-listening.

"Yeah..."

Ruby looks around the dark room, she can make out the vague forms of the objects of Jane and John's lives. She is feeling tired and a little hung over. Her neck hurts with tension.

Five minutes pass in silence. Murrow gives up and goes back to her perch at the windows. Suddenly Mary sits up and stretches and says:

"A cigarette..."

And nothing else. Sayyid Husayn rummages in Mary's purse, finds the Lucky Strikes and lights one for him. Mary smokes and remains withdrawn. He has not taken off his parka. His left hand is in one of its pockets. He is slipping in and out of memories and daydreams of Edith and the times they had together. Mary keeps returning to the spring he convinced Edith to drop out of highschool and take the Greyhound with him to New York City.

It makes Mary feel like shit that he can't stop dwelling on this death and get through it like he has every other loss in his life. How many? How high the stack of corpses? Their familiar and even loved faces stretched out in a line side by side, the violence and the untimeliness of their deaths scratched into their expressions.

Mary knows the Straight Shooters need his active participation in things right now. And he knows there's trouble because of something he's brought down on them. But he just doesn't care. He doesn't.

Mary is not thinking about vengeance for Edith's death. Escape is foremost in his mind. Not to escape from the proximity of his own death, but to flee from the proximity of Edith's. In fact to get out from under the life he's led up to this point in history.

Ruby has given up on her back-and-forth pacing and come to a stop at Murrow's side. Not only is Murrow's nearness reassuring in the usual way but now her pushy opinionated persistence is something Ruby can hold onto. With no words said Murrow has become Mary's successor at Ruby's right hand. She turns and points her hand at Murrow, Marlboro smoldering between her fingers.

"Okay Murrow, go and see if John and Jane's car is still out in front of the Nite Lite. Drive the car back here, around back where I let you all in. If it's not there anymore go to Bontemp's and call me from there."

Murrow starts to go on about the urgency of a counterattack, but Ruby understands that look in her eyes.

"I know Murrow! I fucking know all about it. When you go I'll call Bontemp and Charlie. They'll start working on it.

We'll see how many are left. Then I'll make the move... just get going..."

Murrow pauses at the door and stares at Ruby. But less skeptically than before. She looks at Sayyid Husayn and Mary. She kisses Ruby. Ruby closes the door as she checks her watch.

Out of habit Ruby starts to address herself directly to Mary, catches herself and looks at Sayyid Husayn.

"Husayn. Listen up. There's a small house that the 1st Avenue Tribe uses sometimes, up in Everett. It'll be safe for you two."

Sayyid Husayn almost says he doesn't want safety. Almost says that he's with Murrow and ready for war. But Ruby is boss and Sayyid Husayn retains his trust in her decisions. He also realizes Mary is so far into shock that it'll be a while before he's any good to anybody, especially in a war. He looks at Mary and the fight dribbles out of him. He's a little scared to see Mary so fuckedup. He looks back at Ruby. She makes an effort to relax her face and give him as much encouragement and confidence as she can project right now. Practice for the bigger effort she'll have to make soon enough to a less disciplined crowd. Sayyid Husayn sees the effort she is making more than the leadership she is trying to project and gives in to it. Sayyid Husayn knows what will be coming up for her, especially without Mary there, so he opts to turn around and encourage her by following her lead. He tries the muscle motions that are supposed to create a smile.

"Great. Everett. Where is this?"

"It's about 30 miles north of Seattle."

Mary sits up. He suddenly looks alive for the first time in hours.

"Everett? Where in Everett? Will we be alone? Can we stay there as long as we want?"

Ruby has to admit that she's even more disappointed than she thought she'd be by this reaction. She tries but she just can't look at him.

"It's in Lowell. The redlight district for all those sailors up there... yeah Mary, stay as long as you want..."

Ruby walks to the windows working on another cigarette and wanting a drink. Something straight and up to the rim of the glass. She looks down at the streets, they look wet and cold.

"Like I was telling Husayn. You'll either take the car Murrow's bringing around back or I'll get another. I wrote the directions Eagle Chief gave me on the yellow piece of paper by the telephone. She says you'll find a key in a tupperware pie-slice container buried in front of the bush to the right of door. You know, a triangular-shaped piece of tupperware. For a piece of pie, you know..."

Ruby resumes the pacing. She stops in front of the window she'd stood at last winter and worried about Mary at Clark's Christmas party. She can feel the cold of outside seeping though the glass panes. She pulls her black leather car coat closer and turns back to the two men.

Mary is standing up.

"How long has it been since she left? What if the car isn't there?"

Mary turns and looks at Ruby for a second and then decides against saying anything further. Sayyid Husayn stands up and looks around making sure they've picked up everything of theirs. Mary looks at Ruby again and does not say how much he aches to get out of this city. He only says:

"We'll call your home number and leave a message once we get up there. Then we'll call again tomorrow..."

Mary sticks his hand back in the pocket to make sure Edith's earrings are still there. He makes a quick check of his purse, his revolver is in place. Right now he feels warm and eager and ready to go. He walks over and picks up the paper with their driving directions on it. He scrutinizes them and then says to Sayyid Husayn:

"Got your precious photo?"

Sayyid Husayn nods and pats his topcoat over the area of the suit coat's inner pocket containing the laminated photograph.

"But... my Quran is still in the room..."

Ruby walks over to the two of them.

"I'll send a couple people over and see what we can salvage... you can tell me what you want tomorrow. There's s'posed to be plenty of everything at this place in Lowell..."

Mary starts to say something, Ruby grabs him. They squeeze each other, the phone rings, they aren't strong enough to let go for a long time. The phone rings again. Ruby separates herself from Mary and picks up the receiver.

29

EVERETT

The four small rooms in Lowell are bare except for the basics; stove, fridge, table, a few chairs and a small black-and-white TV. The house is at the far north end of Lowell where there are a few free-standing wood houses left on the perimeter of the Navy- and city-sanctioned sex-industry district. Lowell is officially a part of Everett but has been conveniently cut off from the rest of the city by the wide swath of Interstate 5.

The house is dirty and drafty. They don't do much toward cleaning and spend most of their time around the TV and the fireplace in the main room.

Two weeks go by and they still aren't going outside. Only partly because of any fear of Fiances lurking around. Mostly because Mary doesn't feel well too far from the TV and the liquor. TV or cassettes are always on. There's not much talking.

Couriers come up a couple of times a week with drugs, booze, food, cartons of cigarettes and a little cash but no good news. The bomb in Cigarette shut down everything on that side of the block. 21 dead and 67 injured in the bars, the Oregon Hotel and on the sidewalk outside.

Straight Shooters launch raids into Fiance territory. A few Fiances are killed but nothing much is accomplished. Two fleabag hotels down along Pacific Highway South that the Fiances used as bunkers are torched. Bodies are counted. But there is no real getting ahead for either side.

Police pressure builds toward hysterical media levels. Belltown as hostage. Ruby, Murrow, Charlie and a dozen other Straight Shooters are repeatedly detained for questioning.

Sayyid Husayn is restless. At first he is itchy to get back to Seattle and join the war. But Mary has no enthusiasm for any of it. Mary doesn't give a shit about Seattle anymore. He knows it's over. The war will go on and on. Eventually both sides will be exhausted, resources and loyalties all used up. And Mary figures the Straight Shooters' will run out first.

One night Ruby herself shows up with supplies. She sits across from Mary, watching the flames in the fireplace and tells about her and Murrow's plan to relocate the Straight Shooters. Tacoma, Portland, maybe even Everett. And to them she admits that you don't gain respect and power just by showing up as a crowd in some new city. Besides, there are no other cities that Ruby knows well enough to be able to effectively maneuver in. Murrow is very gung ho about it all. Now that she's the lieutenant her enthusiasm is enough to keep the project going, for the time being.

Mary has only a cursory interest in all this. Sayyid Husayn listens and looks at Ruby and nods and feels the world he's been safe in for these years in Seattle moving away out of his reach.

30

A couple of weeks go by and the war drags on. And the longer it does the more improbable Mary and Sayyid Husayn's return is. And would there be anything worth returning to anyway?

Sayyid Husayn sees something familiar in Mary's shellshock. But at least Mary is also starting to act a little restless. That's a good sign. Sayyid Husayn is definitely getting tired of this bunker mentality. They drink the liquor and do the drugs that are brought. But these stupefiers are not enough.

In a box of stuff salvaged from their room at the Strand, along with the Quran they find a photobooth snapshot of Edith at seventeen. It was from one the first times he'd put on a dress and been convinced to go out with the crew that way. The photo is propped up on the fireplace mantle leaning against the mirror that is on the wall there. The earrings Mary salvaged from his cousin's body are there in front of it. Candles of various sizes and colors are kept lit on both sides of the photo.

Mary stretches and sighs loudly. He gets up and walks from window to window looking out between the drawn curtains. Sayyid Husayn is concentrating on the TV knowing there is not much he can do for his boyfriend

until Mary is ready to let him. Mary has looked out all
the windows, now he stands with his butt to the fire.
Sayyid Husayn looks over and says:

"You... want a drink? Martini?"

Mary doesn't answer. He turns and starts trying to
straighten the part in his hair in the mirror over the
fireplace. He uses a comb on the part and then resets the
barrette on the left side of his head. Mary's eyes shift
from his own face to Edith's picture, back and forth
several times. The candlelight flickers across the dead
man's image trapped in black and white.

"Yeah... yeah a cocktail..."

He starts reapplying his lipstick.

"But not here... we'll go out..."

Sayyid Husayn has no argument with this. He's ready
for them to take their chances in Lowell.

"I was thinking you weren't gonna ask."

Mary stops with the lipstick. He watches his boyfriend
in the mirror. Sayyid Husayn does not look any different
than usual. Was that humor Sayyid Husayn was aiming
for? No, he does not have humor.

"We'll start at the north end of 2nd Avenue and work
our way south until we find a place to plant our fannies
and do some drinking in public."

The project does not take them too long. An hour or so
and they find the right cocktail lounge and they stay put.

The Homeport Steak Place and Cocktail Lounge (Live
Nude Girls 24 Hours).

The Homeport is about halfway down the strip. In the

rest of the month or so they are in Lowell they never bother to go anyplace else. Such a simple-minded strategy, and surprisingly unsound for them to fall into so comfortably.

The lounge itself is designed and decorated like any other. Vinyl-covered booth seats, formica table and countertops, indoor/outdoor carpeting and fake wood paneling. The lighting is vague and dispersed and never changes hour-to-hour day-to-day. A jukebox of current and past Country Western, Golden Oldies, Hard Rock, Heavy Metal and the usual pop. Waitresses with big hairdos, sailors, a few locals and an assortment of female prostitutes. No more no less.

Between the lounge and the restaurant is a wide hallway a dozen and a half yards long. Halfway along it are the swinging double doors that lead into the large room where there are always at least two naked women dancing on a T-shaped stage to a loop of two dozen current Top 40 hits.

They stop at the doorway to the lounge and sniff around for any trouble. The place is nearly empty. Nothing. They sit in one of the smaller booths across from the bar. It is still early evening so everything is nice and quiet. That's fine with Mary and Sayyid Husayn. The fewer new people this first time the better.

To top it all off the first round of Martinis is ice-cold and dry as a desert. After the first couple of sips Sayyid Husayn and Mary become regulars.

31

EVERETT

Mary squashes his smoke and twists around in the chair so that he is facing forward. He nods his head to the rhythm of one of the songs on Lydia Lunch's "13.13." His legs, which had been draped over one of the arms of the chair, swing out and he slams his heels to the floor, stands up, goes to the mirror over the fireplace and reapplies lipstick. He runs his fingers through his hair and wishes he knew somewhere to go for a trim. He could let Sayyid Husayn have a go at it but last time they did that Mary's hair was a mess.

Mary looks at Sayyid Husayn in the mirror. Sayyid Husayn is concentrating on one of the magazines that had been brought up for him. For a while Sayyid Husayn had tried to ration himself, but he has no restraint when it comes right down to it and devours them cover to cover as fast as he can.

The hair will have to do for now. Mary walks to the chair where their coats are draped. When Mary starts to put on his parka and picks up his purse Sayyid Husayn drops the magazine. Mary looks at him.

"I'm bored and I'm sick of this pit... I'm going to the Homeport..."

Mary pulls his parka tightly around him and clutches his handbag to his chest. Sayyid Husayn thinks about it a second and then says:

"We're broke."

"There's a little over four dollars in my purse. We'll have a couple beers at least."

Mary turns to the door, then pauses, his back to Sayyid Husayn.

"What, you don't think I can get someone to buy us Martinis? When *haven't* I gotten us drinks when I put my mind to it?"

"It's Sunday night. Who's gonna be there on a Sunday night?"

"Whatever."

Mary shrugs, walks to the fireplace and again studies his reflection. Sayyid Husayn stands up.

"All-fucking-right. Let me change my shoes, it's pouring out there."

Mary uses a dampened thumb and forefinger to extinguish one of the candles next to Edith's photo. As he pulls his hand away it bumps the candle on the other side of the photo. The liquified wax pooled around the wick gutters off one side and splatters across the already multicolored mosaic of melted-down candles that has built up around the photo.

32

No one is there. No sailors, no other likely punters to cajole or intimidate into buying a round or two. It is still early, but you can pretty much suss out a place right away as to how busy it's likely to get.

Two beers (Rainiers) is two fifty plus the tip and the rest of the change to feed the jukebox. They sit with backs to the wall in one of the big circular booths at the rear of the lounge. A few locals and an occasional sailor drifts back and forth from the restaurant and the nude dancers. They glance at and then ignore the Arab and the transvestite in the back.

Near the jukebox is a table of five women. All of them are waitresses at either the Homeport or one of the other dives along 2nd. All are over 50, with their big hairdos and polyester uniforms and casual wear. They talk loudly and drink steadily. They're either winding down from their shift or getting fortified for their upcoming one.

Squirm around and smoke. An hour later the beers are near their end, very warm and not at all refreshing at this point. A couple of knots of sailors have set themselves up at the bar and the two pool tables, but the place remains empty-feeling. The music selections on the jukebox shift from the Tony Bennett and Frank Sinatra the waitresses had been punching in to rocknroll and current pop. The waitresses are gone now. Even though there are few sailors the people who make their living off them start to show up.

Mary gets a little feeling like maybe if he plays it right he can get something out of one of these boys. But with so few of them the sailors are not as prone to giving him any more than a semi-curious look. No need with the ratio of prostitutes to sailors so much in the sailors' favor. Mary uses his compact and then intently searches the tiny crowd trying to make eye contact with someone. Three of the sailors are Homeport regulars and recognize Mary. Mostly just with quick looks and jokes among buddies. But one of them ventures a quick hello. Sayyid Husayn finishes the tepid backwash of his beer and goes over to the pool tables to see if he can hustle up a game.

Finally it happens, a group of shipmates Mary knows settles into the large booth next to him. They too are regulars and Mary makes a point of greeting each by name. Once the liquor flows and Mary snaps off a string of amusing vulgarities and quips they make a show of inviting him to their table and chatting him up in loud masculine voices. When the booze has done its work they buy him a couple rounds and make (only half-) kidding passes at him.

Mary sits there and takes it all. The drinks and the crude flirting. He has no intention of ending up in bed with any of them, but whatever works to enable a penniless queen to get drunk is just fine with him.

On their way out of the lounge to catch the midnight show of alleged "New and Fresh" dancing girls one of the sailors Mary's been sitting with slips him five dollars with a wink and a leer and a promise of something "real special" someday. Mary smiles at him and in his mind rolls his eyes. Yeah sure, special like dirt is special.

Mary gets up, smooths his skirt and saunters to the bar, checking out the rest of the customers. Leaning on the bar waiting for the bartender Mary dishes with two prostitutes who frequent the Homeport. When he and

Sayyid Husayn first showed up at the Homeport all the women had given him the heavy cold shoulder thinking he was there trying to cut in on the sailor's sex money. Once it was clear he wasn't they'd warmed right up to him. Now the three of them complain about how dull Everett is. The whores wish the Navy'd put the base closer to Seattle so they wouldn't have to spend the time on the Greyhound or money on taxis coming up to Everett and getting back to Seattle.

"No. None of the big ships are due in for at least a week. And this fuckin' rain! None of those pricks wanna take the bus over here, and god forbid they spend money on a cab. Assholes."

"Do either of you know where I can get some decent smoke?"

"Hmm, if Vincent comes in I'll introduce you. I got a dime from him last night that was pretty good."

Once Mary has his drink and some coin change he loiters at the jukebox. He sees Sayyid Husayn has found himself a game with two sailors at one of the pool tables. Mary is torn between sticking with the rocknroll and pop mood that has been on since things got busier, or punching Patsy Cline and Hank Williams Sr. to see what happens. He defers to a sailor for the moment. After watching what the sailor selects Mary decides to stick with rocknroll. It takes Mary a long time to search through all the real drek on the box. So he ends up letting a cute, but impatient, sailor make the last selection for him.

As it turns out the evening's crowd is very temporary, it doesn't last much past 1am. But by this hour Mary has caught a pleasing alcohol buzz. The boredom was never truly relieved, but he managed to get tipsy.

Mary leans back in the booth letting his head droop over to one side. He shakes the coins in his right hand. $2.10. Enough for one last beer with tip and two selections on the jukebox. Mary glances over at Sayyid Husayn and then at the bar. There are three sailors still leaning forward, elbows on the bar. Their butts spread out over three stools in a most unflattering manner. The two on either side leaning inward toward the man in the middle. Periodic sloppy laughter from their huddle.

With his fresh beer in hand Mary heads to the jukebox. Sayyid Husayn intercepts. He has the two sailors he was playing pool with in tow.

"Mary, this is Lewis and this is Davie."

Mary grabs right hands and gives them his vise-squeeze handshake. They respond halfheartedly. One of them does attempt a smile at him, so Mary decides to give them a chance. They go back to the booth and all four slide in. Mary on the far left, then Sayyid Husayn, then Lewis, then Davie.

Lewis is from Detroit and tries to come off with a face of urban confidence and cool. Davie is from a suburb of Sacramento and just watches and drinks beer.

Generally men in the Navy are younger than men in the merchant marine, unless they're officers. So Mary thinks of Navy sailors with thoughts of youth. Unsophisticated (but eager for experience), pushy, hormonal.

These two are nowhere near Mary's 31 years and probably not even to Sayyid Husayn's 23. Lewis is very talkative. His head bobbing back and forth between Sayyid Husayn's face and Mary's. Muscles in his face working furiously as he boasts and chatters.

2 am comes around and Lewis manages to convince Davie to stay with him and go to the little house in the north end of Lowell. Lewis puts out the money for a fifth of Jack Daniel's from the bartender and the four of them trudge up 2nd Avenue.

Sayyid Husayn uses some of Davie's Top tobacco and bits of hashish to roll up some kif. Lewis keeps on with the prattle. Now it's back to his days in highschool. Mary is always sort of shocked when people expose how meaningless and dull their existences have been by extolling highschool as the best years of their lives. Rather frightening when you think about it. Mary pours everyone JDs. Lewis finally catches on that no one gives a shit about highschool and all his buddies and the dreary squalor he likes to think of as adventure. He shuts up and takes a long drink. He looks from Mary to Sayyid Husayn.

"You... uh... guys?... uh..."

Lewis looks back and forth from Mary to Sayyid Husayn unsure if his gender terminology is acceptable. They ignore the question in his tone.

"Uh, you two live here long? Everett I mean. Uh, it's just that you, uh, seem to... know your way around, but uh, you two look kinda outta place in Everett. Know what I mean?..."

"No, we haven't been here long..."

"But too long..."

Mary cracks up at this, Sayyid Husayn manages a smile. Lewis looks confused and Davie is bored. Mary hands Lewis the splif, exhales and waves his hand around.

"This is a friend's place. We're... housesitting..."

The conversation switches to firearms and larger weaponry. With this subject Davie warms up and joins in excitedly. Going on and on about the armaments of the carrier escort they're stationed on. Mary launches into his favorite firearms theme: the utilitarian superiority of revolvers over semiautomatic and automatic handguns. The two sailors scoff, doubting that a man like Mary could have any real knowledge of weaponry. The sailors look at each other and smile indulgently. Seeing he is doubted Mary stops gnashing on his gum, sits back and returns their smiles. Sayyid Husayn looks at Mary and then the guests. He rubs a thumbnail on his gold tooth. Mary says:

"Alright boys. Let's have a little contest. Breaking down, cleaning and reassembling my Smith & Wesson .38. Hmm? And you two can show us just how well-trained you are..."

Davie gets a doubtful uneasy look on his chubby face. He looks to Lewis for reassurance and then takes a strong swig (from the jar he is using as a glass) of Jack Daniel's. Lewis is confused again. He looks into his drink and then bursts out laughing and pounds the table top with the palm of his hand. Mary and Sayyid Husayn grab for their own drinks as his pounding shakes the flimsy table.

"You guys are too much! Too much! Fuckin'-A! Hey, let me pour another round."

He grabs the neck of the fifth and splashes whiskey in all four glasses (actually two jars and two glasses). For the first time that night Lewis holds Mary's gaze for longer than 2 seconds. Lewis nudges Davie as he says:

"Shit, if he was a girl... shit..."

He gives Davie the conspiratorial wink and nod. He looks Mary up and down.

"... if you were a girl... I'd be in your pants so fast... before you could say — dirty dancing!"

Mary stops chewing his gum. Sayyid Husayn is choking on a mouthful of whiskey. Without looking at Sayyid Husayn Mary reaches over and squeezes his leg.

"But honey, I'm not wearing pants..."

Lewis blinks then laughs and again jostles the table with his pounding. Davie doesn't react. If he knew how to sneer, and didn't think it was too faggoty, he would have. Lewis stops laughing and is obviously restless, shifting around in his seat. One hand is on his drink and the other is under the table squeezing his crotch. Sayyid Husayn sees this and tries not to stare. Lewis says:

"Shit, I wish there were more good-looking chicks in this town. No offense you guys, but I could sure use some of that soft and round stuff..."

Sayyid Husayn wonders what this man really wants hanging around with them. Sayyid Husayn thinks of the Homeport. Tonight there were at least five or six women in the place who would've done something quick and effective for 20, 30 bucks. For five bucks Lewis could have gotten into the go-go show, sat in one of the booths that ring the stage, and if he was discreet, jacked off. Sailors are always looking for a good time. Sayyid Husayn wonders if they ever have any.

Sayyid Husayn knows sailors sometimes carry a lot of cash and are always acting horny. He is buddy-buddy with this one prostitute Maureen, and he figures between her and Mary they could get these boys in a position where they would be easy to rip off.

But Mary likes Lewis. He likes him in the passing way he appreciates men who are not afraid of him but who are not a part of his everyday life. Lewis is the kind of man who hasn't really taken care of himself but his body is still young enough, and awash with hormones, to strongly signify masculinity. Not that youth and testosterone amount to a whole lot really. But on Lewis, at 21, his plainness and youth work for him, image-wise.

Sayyid Husayn knows this is how Mary sees Lewis, but he really doesn't understand it. He never bothers with all the sorting and characterizing of people that Mary seems to find so vital in delineating the world. If a person isn't someone Sayyid Husayn has allowed into his small circle of friends then he doesn't bother to remember them let alone contemplate or try to understand them. These outsiders do not even signify "nothing" to him. They do not signify. Sometimes they are stupid or mean or cruel and he has to kill them.

33

Davie never does come back and they only see him in passing at the Homeport. But Lewis comes around to their place or meets up with them in the lounge quite a bit for the next couple of weeks. A few times he just stops by their table to say hello with women he's hired and then takes off to make use of them. He brings these women by as if he is seeking Mary and Sayyid Husayn's approval or understanding. As if Mary and Sayyid Husayn are his betters in some way.

Lewis usually drops by their house whenever he's on shore leave. Smoking their hashish and Mexican black tar heroin. In exchange he is usually the one who pays for the drinks when they go out.

34

EVERETT – SEATTLE – EVERETT

The lights are off and the TV is a flashing illumination behind him. Mary stares at the photo of Edith and at the pair of earrings Edith wore on the night he was killed. Candlelight shifting and wavering over his forever young and two-dimensional face. Mary starts thinking back a half dozen or so years to when he and Edith were spending a lot of weekend nights hanging around Pioneer Square. Hawks circling and circling the various yuppie bars and restaurants of that neighborhood, eyes on the tender and well-to-do.

They follow this one couple in pastels and blowdried haircuts a few blocks to a BMW (silver and blue) parked along a side street. As they move in Mary is saying to Edith:

"Pick up the pace... never let'm get too far ahead. Never give'm a chance to try and unlock the car doors. Minimize situations where you gotta start shooting to control things. Some of these shits keep pieces in the glove box or under the car seat — and some of them are fucking dumb enough to try and go for it..."

Click click click, heels on asphalt getting closer to the targets. The man's a little more drunk than the woman. He fumbles for his keys. She looks up and stares. Mary and Edith are just a couple of yards away now. Mary gears up for action. He thinks she might be trouble. That taking-it-all-in no-nonsense look on her face. Edith takes two steps to Mary's right and has his Colt 9mm up and ready. Gripping it with both hands, elbows slightly bent. Edith glances up, gauging the streetlight's position overhead and shuffles half a step or so back so that it shows him in a more flattering light. He settles back into his pose.

The woman grabs the man's arm and tries to pull him to the back of the BMW. He looks at her confused and then turns, following her stare to the two transvestites.

Mary raises his left hand gesturing for the two yuppies to stop.

"Nice and easy, nice and easy. Stay put and be nice... both of ya..."

Edith is grinning and wide-eyed. He giggles. Mary flashes a smile. Just to let them know who's in control. He likes how his cousin gets the slightly psycho look and starts grinning that way when they do a crime. Keeps the punters nervous. Crazy dragqueen with a gun.

Man looking scared. Woman glaring, irritated.

"Okay. Empty your pockets. Hand me the purse."

The man stuffs his hands in his pants pockets but the woman squeezes his arm to make him stop. She turns and full faces them. Yeah she could be trouble Mary thinks. The woman says:

"What the fuck are you two doing?... There's people everywhere..."

Edith giggles. Mary makes a show of casually looking up and down the block in both directions and seeing nobody. He looks at her, tilts his head. His .38 is loose at his side, his thumb slowly rubbing the butt.

"Don't get started sister. You got guts. Great. So there's no need to get 'em spilled on the sidewalk. Your purse."

Edith has been looking the man up and down.

"Hey, honey. I know you, don't I? Ya, you hunky thing. The Six Eleven. Right?"

Edith giggles after saying this. The woman scoffs and looks at the man. Waiting for him to stand up for himself. The man looks from her to Edith. Mary watches the man and for a second wonders if Edith is telling the truth. The man looks back at the woman, panic in his eyes. He can see she is expecting something out of him but he is more afraid of the man in the dress with the gun. He stammers:

"Uh... I don't think so..."

"Oh no, I'm sure I seen you at the Six Eleven. You were busy in the men's room. Uh, third stall from the door wasn't it? Right? Say I'm right."

"Uh, no. I... no..."

He's definitely scared now. The woman glances from Edith to him. Edith keeps it up.

"Sweet-thing, come on with us. Can you handle the two of us? I'll teach you something real fun..."

Mary is ignoring Edith's badgering. He is keeping his eyes on the woman. He hopes she does not try anything heroic-like.

"Alright shut up Edith. He'll end up pissing his pants if you keep it up.... Both of you empty your pockets... and I'm still waiting for the purse."

The woman hands over her small purse and curses her date. The man is shaking a little. He fumbles through his pockets. The woman moves several paces to one side putting space between herself and her now ex-date. She stands with her arms folded across her chest.

The take is minimal. Mary demands the guy's Rolex. Mary studies the woman a minute. Her jaw clenches and unclenches. Mary takes a 10 from the roll and hands it to her. She looks at it and then him. Mary shakes it at her and gestures with his head at the man cowering beside his BMW.

"Ten bucks. So you can take a cab."

She looks at Mary and then the man. She snatches the money and stuffs it in her pocket, glares at the man. Mary returns her purse and then she strides away down the street.

Edith laughs out loud. He lowers his semiautomatic.

"Now, are you sure you don't wanna come with us? I mean, you ain't gonna get nothing from her now are you? Like I said I can show you something real fun, I mean like real fun, baby. Trust me."

The man is staring at the sidewalk. Mary taps Edith on the shoulder and they take off.

Mary smiles while he thinks back on this and other incidents. It never pulled in much, but it was usually good for a laugh and a story for back at the Frontier Room.

Mary leans back and laughs to himself. Sayyid Husayn's eyes leave the TV screen and he glances a second at his boyfriend and then back at the screen. Mary laughs again. Imagining that schmuck on his hands and knees on the dirty damp tile of the men's room of the Six Eleven.

The next time Mary and Edith are in the Six Eleven Edith keeps saying things like:

"There he is. The one in the chartreuse hot pants..."

And.

"Isn't that him? The one that biker's groping?"

Five, six years ago. Mary looks at the TV, at Sayyid Husayn and then his eyes linger on the black-and-white photobooth picture on the fireplace mantle. One candle has burned out. The other sputters and the light flickers across Edith's frozen face.

35

EVERETT

One muggy June afternoon when Mary is not awake yet Lewis and Sayyid Husayn are sitting in the main room drinking coffee and watching TV. Lewis starts up with the complaining (again) about having no place of his own to bring "girls" to. And how the motels in the area are always jacking up the price of a room as soon as they think a guy's a sailor. He shakes his head with disgust. He sits on the chair with his feet up on the brick of the fireplace.

"So... like... uh, I was wondering, if there was some-way I could, uh, bring a girl, uh, here — only sometimes I mean! You know... I'd give you say, 10... 20 bucks each time. Hey, I know you're getting it nice and regular Husayn, but me, I can't hardly afford the girl and the motel room to do her in... whaddaya say?"

Sayyid Husayn considers it. He thinks of asking for $25. If it were just once or twice a week it might be a tolerable arrangement. He knows Mary will get a kick out of it. Sayyid Husayn's only qualm is the notion of two other people fucking on the bed he has to sleep in.

But sheets can be changed. Sayyid Husayn does not like Lewis very much, and this pathetic request just reinforces how really little that is. Sayyid Husayn studies Lewis to make sure he's as serious and desperate as he acts. Lewis gives him a little-boy anxiety look that makes Sayyid Husayn want to spit on him. So he grins slyly and instead of asking for extra money he says:

"Well Lewis, you can keep your 10 dollars. How about this instead. Just let me and Mary watch. Know what I mean? We'd stay way back out of the way of course. We wouldn't say or do anything. Just watch. What the fuck, most of the pro's aren't gonna give a shit..."

Sayyid Husayn speaks in a low insinuating tone never taking his eyes off Lewis. Lewis doesn't say anything, he laughs weakly. Sayyid Husayn can see he'll do it, but to sweeten the deal he says:

"And listen, we've got this big mirror right next to the bed... Mary and I like it... could be real fun for you... understand what I'm saying?"

At this suggestion Lewis drops his look of discomfort. He pretends not to have heard the part about Sayyid Husayn and Mary being spectators.

"Shit! A mirror?! That'd be fucking outrageous Husayn! What a rush..."

For a moment Lewis is lost in fantasy. He smiles and saliva gathers at the corners of his mouth.

"So, you and Mary, uh, use this mirror huh? I bet that's really something..."

Sayyid Husayn shrugs noncommittally. Lewis sits back, lifts his butt off the couch and digs around in his pants' pockets. He pulls out a bunch of folded money.

"Okay, look here's like, uh, a down payment..."

"No, no. Keep your money. Just let us watch. Okay?"

Now it's Lewis' turn to shrug. He squirms and then sheepishly says:

"Alright guy. You wanna... watch, okay. You two can't be making no sideline comments..."

Lewis chuckles lewdly.

"Yeah, yeah. No comments. But you gotta call us before you come over. Better yet, call us a day before you wanna use the bed... and mirror. Okay? I don't want you just showing up at our door with some woman expecting to use the bed right then. Got it? Okay?"

"Sure, sure man. Hey that's cool. I'm no jerk."

The corner of Sayyid Husayn's mouth convulses with a momentary sneer.

Lewis fades back into fantasizing. He wipes the palms of his now sweating hands on his acid-washed blue jeans and shakes his head.

"Shit, shit, shit... just thinking about that mirror is making me so fucking horny... can I take a look at it?"

"No. Mary's still asleep in there."

Lewis rubs his palms on his jeans again. Sayyid Husayn decides to play with him further.

"But let's put it this way. The mirror is nice and big. You can see everything. It's attached to the dresser so you can't be moving it around. You have to shove the bed around until you can see things how you want... you know, the angle that is just right..."

"Whatever man..."

"And don't go breaking the fucking mirror, this place isn't ours you know..."

"Okay, okay! Come on, stop talking about it! It's getting me all bothered... maybe I could, uh, use it tomorrow?..."

"Yeah, maybe. We'll have to talk to Mary."

"Sure, sure, Mary's cool. He'll let me do it. Hey, do you really think Mary wants to watch me giving it to some babe? Does he, you know, like me?"

"Oh yeah, he likes you..."

"Shit..."

Lewis stands up, gulps down the last of his coffee and says:

"Let's go get a pint of something good to start the evening off with. When we get back maybe Mary will be awake and I can take a look at the bedroom."

He looks at his watch.

"Damn. Come on, I gotta be back on board at 23:00."

"Alright. Let me go look in on Mary."

36

SPOKANE

It is the middle of the night. But it is not completely dark in Harvey's bedroom. The streetlight gives the room a dull flat illumination. The room is quiet but for the sleep breathing of the two people in the bed.

Harvey suddenly sits bolt upright in the bed. He had been very dead asleep. He rubs his eyes, trying to focus on the telephone on the dresser across the room. He rummages around on the floor next to the bed for his underwear or Levis' but he can't find either. Harvey looks at the phone again and then crawls over to it. Standing and fumbling a second he finally picks up the receiver. His voice is rough and gravelly with sleep.

"Hello?..."

But there is only dial tone. The phone had not rung. At all. Harvey moves the receiver from his ear and stares at it. He looks back at the bed and then again at the phone receiver in his hand. The dial tone ends and a prerecorded voice comes on.

"If you'd like to make a call please hang up and dial again. If you need help please hang up and dial your operator..."

Then there is a series of harsh electronic tones and Harvey jerks the receiver farther from his face and stares at it.

The receiver clatters back into the cradle. Harvey stumbles back to the bed. The girl in the bed stirs, stretches but does not waken. Harvey gets in and starts to pull the covers up when the phone rings.

Harvey drops the blankets, turns and stares at the phone. It rings again. Now the girl starts to rouse. Harvey sighs and gets out of bed.

"It's the phone. I'll get it. Go back to sleep."

This time when he picks it up there is no dial tone. He says nothing and listens. On the other end of the line he can hear The Doors playing in the background.

"Harvey? Harvey? It's Sheila..."

"Sheila? Hello? Uh, did you just call me? I mean a minute ago?"

"Hmm? No, no... Harvey, listen. A week, maybe less, maybe 10 days... and She'll be here! 10 days! D'ya hear me? Harvey? I said maybe a week, maybe 10 days and The Lady'll be here..."

Now Harvey is wide awake. He is shivering in the cold but all his attention is on what Sheila has said. His grip on the black plastic phone receiver tightens.

"A week, 10 days? What the fuck should we be doing? Should I get the others together at the grotto? What time is it?..."

Harvey is pulling out dresser drawers and searching for clothes to put on.

"No, no Harvey... .It's, uh, after four... no, don't call anyone else... I was just laying here listening to The Doors and saying the Rosary... and then She whispers in my ear that She's ready to come see us...

"As soon as She left I had the feeling I should call and tell you..."

Harvey drops the briefs and socks he'd managed to find back into a drawer. The adrenaline begins to fade. He stretches. He is smiling.

"Yeah, thanks Sheila, I 'preciate it... what time should we get together tomorrow?"

"Oh... same time. I'm not going to school so I'll be at the grotto all day. You can come over when you want... I just wanted you to know Harvey. Okay I'm gonna try and go to sleep... you should go back to sleep... call me in the morning, I probably won't leave here 'til noon..."

"Yeah, g'night Sheila... thanks for the call..."

"G'night Harvey."

Dial tone again. Harvey sets the phone down. The girl has spread herself out into the middle of the bed and gone back to sleep. Harvey has to prod her over to one side so he can get in.

Harvey can't sleep. He lies there thinking. A week maybe. Maybe 10 days and the whole world changes forever. His body is warming up under the blankets but he shivers with pleasure. Harvey believes Her Manifestation will expose the purpose of his life.

The immediacy of the Mystery of Her Arrival is so exciting Harvey cannot sleep. This excitement is very sexual to him. He does not know why but Her closeness causes his penis to slowly fill and pulsate with blood. Harvey turns onto his side so he faces the girl who'd picked him up at the concert earlier that night. Slowly he starts running the palm of his left hand up and down the length of her body. Hopefully she will wake up and want to fuck again.

37

EVERETT

In mid-July the phone rings and it's Lewis. He's shipping out in a few hours and wants to say goodbye. He's known for a week that his ship is leaving, but he was afraid to tell them for fear they'd reject him, maybe cut off his bed-and-mirror privileges. Sayyid Husayn can hear Lewis' apologetic whine coming over the line. Mary hangs up after a noncommittal goodbye. He rolls his eyes and shrugs.

"Sometimes these boys... sometimes they are so fucking..."

"He's an asshole. I told you we shoulda rolled him when we had the chance."

"Rolled him for what? He never had more than 50 or 60 bucks on him at any one time."

"And what are we s'posed to do with all those Polaroids he left here? Keep 'em as souvenirs? Tokens of his friendship?"

For a while Lewis had been a distraction from the tedium of their exile. Now, again, there is nothing. The occasional visitor from Seattle. But these visits are too few, too short and bring them only bad news. Ruby comes up a couple of times, but she has her hands full organizing the daydream of mass migration. Ruby decides her friend got himself into this, let him worm his way out of this, if he can.

38

"Alright."

Mary drops the last of the coins he's counting into his

palm. He looks from the coins to the paper money on the table and calculates.

"We've got enough for two cocktails apiece. Let's go."

The extended boredom has made Sayyid Husayn cranky and uncooperative.

Mary doesn't bother waiting for answer. He puts on shoes. He decides it's probably warm enough this evening that he doesn't need a jacket of any kind. Sayyid Husayn finally gets to his feet and starts to dress.

"All my trousers are wrinkled."

"Fuck you. I told you to iron them days ago."

Sayyid Husayn mutters something in Arabic.

HOMEPORT – STEAKS – COCKTAILS – LIVE – NUDE – GIRLS – 24 – HOURS. The multicolored neon sign lights up from top to bottom, one word at a time. The whole sign then flashes on and off three times, then goes dark and starts the sequence all over again.

At the door to the go-go show Mary and Sayyid Husayn pause. Standing in just the right place they can see through the space between the swinging doors and catch glimpses of the women as they shake and wiggle on the T-shaped stage. Rotating color wheels in front of the spotlights splash the women's nakedness with waves of color, none of which are very flattering on them.

As they move into the lounge Mary's sleeveless white sweater briefly glows blue as he passes under the black light above the entranceway.

Lewis' ship is not the only one headed out. The restaurant, go-go showroom and lounge are nearly empty. One of the two waitresses leaning on the bar comes dashing over as soon as they slide into a booth.

"Hey kids, what's up. Man this place is a fuckin' drag tonight! Some dumbfuck OD'd in the men's room and I've barely pulled in enough tips for a cab home. So, has your sailor boy left with the rest of 'em?"

"Yeah. I guess. He said something about the coast of Peru. I dunno. Some part of the War On Drugs. Whatever. Good riddance."

Mary piles the crumpled bills and coins on the table top. The waitress scans their meager funds and shrugs resignedly.

"Oh well, I wasn't planning on going to Hawaii tomorrow anyway. What'llya have? The usual, very dry and very cold?"

"No, I think... for me, Gin and Tonic."

"Yeah, me too."

"Ooh, really living on the edge tonight aren't we."

Once the drinks arrive neither of them picks theirs up right away. With the place this dead there's no real chance of cadging any drinks. So they let the drinks sit, trying to stretch out the evening as best they can. Sayyid Husayn slouches back in the booth smoking and blowing smoke rings. Mary is also smoking. With his free hand Mary fishes out the wedge of lime from his drink, squeezes the juice into the Gin and Tonic and drops the wedge back in. He stabs his index finger down into the drink and stirs. This done Mary takes a sip. Satisfied with its taste he replaces the glass on the paper cocktail napkin and joins his boyfriend in leaning back and watching the TV over the bar. Mary considers plugging a few quarters into the jukebox, but this will not leave a decent tip for the second round. Mary sighs loudly. Sayyid Husayn ignores or does not hear this.

Mary looks at his boyfriend. Sayyid Husayn is wrapped up in a copshow. When a criminal shoots a cop in the face a small smile pulls at Sayyid Husayn's lips, briefly exposing crooked yellowed teeth. As the cop lies dying Sayyid Husayn stops his persistent fiddling with a matchbook cover and concentrates entirely on the TV screen. Once the cop is definitely dead he leans back, takes a final draw on his cigarette and smashes it out in the ashtray. Holding up his drink he studies it a second and then gulps down half. Mary follows suit. No use waiting too long, the drink'll just get watery and warm. Mary sits back waiting for the liquor to warm his stomach.

The second wave of Gin and Tonics arrive. At their request the waitress makes sure the bartender mixes these drinks in the same glasses as the first. This is a common request among regulars at the Homeport that is meant to save you from having to put up with the dishwasher soap taste of the clean glasses.

With the tip paid there's still 30 cents in nickels and pennies stacked on the formica-topped table. Mary digs out his small red plastic-covered address book. He flips from page to page scrutinizing the crowd of scribbled entries. He is looking for a name and address in some other city (anywhere — if only he knew someone in Fargo, North Dakota...). Some destination that could be a direction to head in. Mary knows plenty of people in cities all over the the United States, but nothing stands out as useful in their current circumstances.

Sayyid Husayn swallows half of his second cocktail, sets it down and resumes with the empty matchbook cover he's been folding end over end, then unfolding and refolding in the opposite direction. This endless repetitive fidgeting is starting to bug Mary. He points to the small stack of coins near the ashtray.

"Why don'tcha trade these in for some dimes and go feed the jukebox."

When Sayyid Husayn gets back to the table Madonna is belting out one of her old hits. Mary has given up on his address book, no leads there. It is resting facedown near Mary's drink. As soon as Sayyid Husayn is settled into the booth he reaches for the matchbook but Mary is quicker and snatches it up.

"What the fuck is it with you and this matchbook!"

Mary unfolds it all the way and glances at both sides disinterestedly. He starts to drop it back on the table, out of Sayyid Husayn's reach. He stops and brings the inside of the matchbook closer to his face so he can see something on it more clearly. The dim lighting of the lounge makes it difficult and he has to concentrate for a minute to discern what is there. Despite the series of deep folds running the width of the matchbook Mary can see there are a few words printed on it in blue ball-point pen.

"Did you write this?"

"What?"

"This here, in blue ball-point."

Mary puts the inside of the matchbook nearer Sayyid Husayn's face. Sayyid Husayn squints trying to make it out.

"US 2 TO I-90... SPOKANE... EXIT 282..."

Sayyid Husayn pronounces the city "Spō-kān." He reads the writing in the matchbook out loud again and shakes his head.

"No. I just picked it up when we sat down. It was laying next to the ashtray when we got here. I wasn't paying any attention, just folding it."

Mary looks at the words again.

"Spokane. That's in eastern Washington. On the other side of the Cascades. Edith and Ruby and me used to drive over there a couple times a year to do thrift shopping. Spokane was good shopping."

"Suits? Ever see any good suits in Spokane?"

"You say it 'Spō-kǎn.' "

"Spokane, whatever. Were there good suits in — Spokane?"

"Men's suits were not something any of us were looking at."

Mary sets the matchbook on the table, propping it up against his glass so he can still sort of see the handwriting. Sayyid Husayn takes another large gulp of Gin and Tonic.

Sayyid Husayn is sitting upright and his voice has an edge of excitement.

"So, those are like what, directions to some city? Or some place in a city? In, Spokane?"

"Yeah. US 2 and Interstate 90 are highways and Exit 282 must be somewhere in Spokane, I guess. I don't remember the city that well. I guess we always took I-90 there. Yeah, I'm pretty sure."

Sayyid Husayn grips Mary's shoulder, his eyes are bright and his voice is filled with awe, like the words in blue ball-point are in God's own handwriting.

"It's, uh, a... clue! No, it's, uh lead. Right? A place to go to. Isn't that what you were looking for in your book? A way out of this dump. God provides.

"I mean we're never gonna be able to go back to Seattle are we? And if we did, it's not gonna be the place we made home is it? And Everett is a pit. I can't take it here much longer. We have to follow these directions, this lead. God willing, something can happen to us. It's our chance Mary..."

Sayyid Husayn sits back, staring into space. Dreaming of suits no doubt.

"God willing," "God provides," Mary thinks with irritation. Mary's eyes unfocus and he also wonders about Spokane. It could be a start. There might be some work for men with their skills. It wouldn't be hard to get some cash together. Ruby would probably get them a car. Maybe even John and Jane's sedan. Such a nice car for traveling in.

Besides if they're out on the road on their own Ruby and Murrow wouldn't feel so obligated to keep an eye on them. The Straight Shooters could concentrate on hitting the Fiances hard enough to keep them out of Belltown until Ruby can give this evacuation thing a try.

And if Spokane is nothing, they can just keep going east and/or south. Mary considers the handwritten words on the inside of the matchbook.

"Okay. Sure. Spokane. Let's go home and I'll call Ruby and see what she can do about a car and some money. You can start packing."

Mary puts his address book away, Sayyid Husayn downs the rest of his drink and scoots out of the booth. Mary stuffs the matchbook into his small change purse and finishes his own drink.

39

EVERETT–PORTLAND

"Hello?"

"Hi there mom. It's me, your son Robert..."

"Robbie! I was wondering when I was going to hear from you..."

Mary's mother turns from the mouthpiece of her phone and yells to her mother who is in another room.

"Ma! It's Robbie..."

Mary hears his grandmother yelling back in an unsteady but excited voice. He visualizes her pushing herself up out of the ratty old easy chair in the living room of the little yellow house in Portland, Oregon. He can see her pulling her sweater closer and moving as quickly as her small steps allow to the phone in the hall.

His mother puts the receiver to her mouth again.

"Robert, how are you honey? How's that boy of yours Husayn? You're keeping him fed I hope. We really enjoyed his visit a couple months ago.... So, are you two working at all?..."

"Mom, we're always workin'..."

"Hmm, you know what I mean Robert. Something... steady..."

"Yeah mom, I know... we're doin' fine mom."

"Anyway honey it's so good to hear your voice. Any chance both of you will come visit us anytime soon? You know we'd love to have both you boys for a while..."

"No, not anytime soon.... It's getting hot up here. You two keeping cool?"

"Oh, you know. This place always stays pretty comfy unless it gets over 90.

"Robert, your grama still won't listen to me about these walks she takes. I try to keep an eye on her, but no matter what the temperature is she is still goes out every afternoon. Even when it's ungodly hot or pouring rain. Sure sometimes she only walks as far as Mildred Burser's front porch. But some days, oh my god, some days she goes all the way up to the bus stop on Bayridge! Bayridge Street! She sits there for hours! In all kinds of weather! Thankgod there's a roof over the bus stop! She sits there for hours! Watching the people she tells me! Talking with god knows who! I've told her I'm too old to be chasing after her. What if something happens to her?"

Mary hears his grandmother scoff loudly in the background.

"Judith Pellmand — you know, the woman with all those poodles — well she lives right kitty-corner from that bus stop. But I can't expect Judith to keep an eye on Margaret all day. And what if she gets on a bus and ends up god knows where!"

"Mom! You're treating Margaret like she's senile or something! Sometimes I think she's saner than you are. I don't want you giving her such a hard time. Do ya hear me mom? Do ya? Let her live a life jesuschrist. You took her to that doctor and she said Margaret is just fine. Be nice or I'll come down there and get her and bring her up here to live with Husayn and me..."

Caught up in their conversation Mary has forgotten about his current circumstances and why he was calling in the first place. He looks around the main room of the ugly little house in Everett and grimaces. His mother interrupts his mood.

"Yeah, yeah. You're so worried about how I treat my mother — what about you? Are you at least coming down here for my birthday? It's two weeks away."

Mary pulls a cigarette out of its pack and Sayyid Husayn leans forward and lights it for him. Mary tries to remember what they'd gotten his mother for her birthday last year.

"Sorry mom. We can't get to Portland that soon. But Husayn and I got you something you'll really like. I'll send it off in a week or so. And I don't want you opening it before your birthday."

"You know I always open packages as soon as they arrive. Besides, what I'd really like is a new photo of

Husayn and you. That one I have is at least two years old."

Mary sits up straight. The idea of getting dressed up and going to some photobooth and getting a bunch of pictures right at this juncture in their lives is very appealing.

"Yeah. Okay, we'll try and do it soon.

"Oh yeah, uh mom, Husayn and I, we're gonna take a trip in a couple days. I'm not sure when we'll be back... I'll send you postcards along the way."

"You two flying?"

"No mom, we're not flying. You know I hate planes. We got a nice car. We're gonna take our time, see the sights, y'know."

"Robbie you have to be sure and take lots of pictures. Your dad and I always took lots of pictures on our vacations.

"You remember the photos from that trip you, me, dad, Aunt Arlene, your Uncle David and Scott took to California? That time when we went down to Monterey, when Margaret and your grandfather still lived there? Hmm, that was one of the best vacations your dad and I ever had. Even with everyone else along. Remember how Uncle David didn't want to go and ended up having such a good time..."

Mary loses track of what his mother is saying. Mention of Edith's parents has sent his mind off remembering. A shuffling stack of images of Edith at sixteen or seventeen, all worked up because he can't get the makeup on right and because the skirt he's wearing makes him look scrawny and hipless.

"Robert? Robert honey, are you there? What's wrong? Did you hear what I was saying?"

"Mom... I gotta tell you something... just listen to me mom... Scott... Edith, he's dead mom. He was in a bar, and some people got in a fight and they had guns... and, Edith was in the way. He got shot mom... I thought maybe you woulda already known... the city is holding his body I think..."

There is silence in Portland and in Everett. Sayyid Husayn has been sitting nearby throughout the conversation. He's always felt very close to Mary's mother and grandmother. Sayyid Husayn scans Mary's face trying to detect how Sylvia is taking the news. He's never met Edith's parents, David and Arlene, so he is mostly worried about how Margaret and Sylvia will handle it.

Mary's jaw is clenched, his lips are a tight line. His mother's shocked silence stokes and feeds Mary's apathetic glare.

Sayyid Husayn stands up and reaches for the phone. "Here, let me talk to Sylvia."

40

SPOKANE

The day has been very, very hot. Spokane has been smothering in heat since they arrived two days ago. Mary is quite content to spend this day behind drawn curtains in their air-conditioned motel room. The difference between the rainy temperate climate of Seattle and the arid heat of Washington east of the Cascade mountains seems extremely harsh to Mary. He remembers now why they didn't make shopping excursions over here very often. Mary'd put up with the heat and glaring sun yesterday to go thrift shopping. Today he wants to stay in front of the color TV, have a few cocktails and lounge until the sun goes down.

Sayyid Husayn is restless. This kind of weather reminds him of home and he hasn't seen much of it in recent years. The beautiful torrential heat and sun.

Sayyid Husayn changes suits. He puts his revolver back in its shoulder holster over a clean white short sleeve shirt. He has decided to go out on his own for a walk.

He steps out into the motel's parkinglot and adjusts his sunglasses. He walks for a long time, most of the afternoon. Spokane is nice and hot but doesn't seem any more interesting than Everett.

On his way back to the motel Sayyid Husayn decides to go into the cafe he and Mary had stopped in yesterday to eat lunch. Sitting in one of the booths in the back he orders three pieces of pie. One of each kind available. And coffee to go with them.

Harvey is aimlessly swirling a spoon in a cup of coffee. The door of the cafe opens, the bell over the door jingles. Harvey looks up for the 50th time that day. Instantly Harvey recognizes that this man in a light gray suit is The Lady's Companion. Just like he remembers Him from yesterday, only His suit is different. Harvey gets Harriet's attention and she zooms over to get The Companion's order. Harvey tries to watch without being too obvious. It's hard to tell whether The Companion has noticed him. He is wearing the same sunglasses as yesterday.

Harriet's had this job waiting tables on weekends and Mondays for quite a while now. Yesterday she was ringing up a check, the door opens and Mary and Sayyid Husayn walk in and sit down in a booth. She brings them menus. She can't stop staring.

This is Her. It is so obvious, this is Our Lady. The shorter skinny guy must be Her Companion; some sort of angel too no doubt. Harriet goes back into the kitchen and stands there shaking all over. She can't believe it is happening to her. To have Our Lady of the Ugly Ones appear to her first of all. It scares Harriet. Her and all her doubts. Thinking like she did that the way the others carry on is pretty stupid sometimes. But there She is right in booth five.

It's just like Sheila said it would be. Out of the blue. In the most unlikely of places. And here They are, having lunch. Two cheeseburgers with fries, coffees, and Her Companion wants a piece of apple pie and a piece of peach pie.

After the initial shock Harriet gives Their order to the cook and goes to the payphone by the restrooms. She drops the quarter as she tries to get it in the slot. She dials the wrong number and has to go get another quarter. Harriet gets ahold of Harvey and she stammers out who she thinks has come into the cafe. They decide Harvey should come over and check it out before they call Sheila and the others. Both of them are sort of worried about how Sheila will react if this really is Her.

Harvey comes in and sits at the counter. He tries to discreetly keep an eye on the transvestite and the Arab as they eat their lunch. It takes about five minutes for Harvey to finally decide for sure that Harriet is right. This is Her. He looks at his wristwatch so he can memorize the hour and the date it happened.

Harvey uses the same payphone Harriet had to call Raeann's. He knows Sheila is likely to be there. But before Sheila can get to the cafe The Lady and Her Companion pay their check and leave. Harvey is frantic, almost in tears. He waited too long before calling Sheila. He has to restrain himself from jumping up in front of the door.

When Sheila gets there and the Two are gone she is entirely nonplussed. She and the five others squeeze into the booth where They had just been. Sheila gets to sit where Our Lady had. The vinyl is still warm from Their bodies. Sheila smiles.

"... at least one of us will be here all the time the cafe is open for business. So when They return we'll be ready..."

Sheila is so matter-of-fact that none of the others think to question her on how they're going to have someone here from six in the morning 'til three in the morning, or whether They will come back to this particular cafe.

Harvey manages not to openly run past The Companion to the payphone in back. He calls Sheila and then Raeann's. They are designated to gather the others. 15 minutes and everyone is perched along the counter trying not to stare.

Sayyid Husayn eats a piece of pie then smokes a cigarette, eats a second piece of pie and smokes another cigarette. He never removes his sunglasses. After the third piece of pie (cherry) and a third cigarette he gives Harriet his check and some money. While she is ringing it up Sayyid Husayn sits and drinks coffee. When Harriet returns with the change he thanks her and finishes his coffee. He gets up, fishes some more coins from his trouser pocket and leaves them with the change from his bill for a tip, and then goes to the men's room.

Without thinking about it Harvey jumps down and follows Him. Harvey hesitates two heartbeats at the door then pushes it open and walks to the urinal to the left of where The Companion is standing.

But Sayyid Husayn isn't peeing. He is well aware that something is up, that he was being watched. He recognized the kid sitting at the counter and the waitress when he first came in, they were both here yesterday. Halfway through his pie four other kids show up who are obviously friends of the first two. They do a piss-poor job of hiding the fact that they are watching him as he eats. He decides to see if someone will follow him into the bathroom. The guy from the day before does.

Sayyid Husayn turns and stares at the boy from behind ray-bans.

"What the fuck do you kids want? You and that redhead were both here yesterday. What do you want?..."

His voice is quiet and clipped and it scares the shit out of Harvey.

"Nothing man, nothing... I just gotta piss... really..."

Sayyid Husayn says nothing. He doesn't believe the boy. Sayyid Husayn studies him. The kid is muscular but doesn't act tough, doesn't look like he is accustomed to using his muscle for violence. He doubts these kids are any sort of threat. They could be some sort of scouts for the Fiances, but they sure aren't doing a very good job of reconnaissance. Sayyid Husayn considers killing the boy right here. He wonders if they followed him and Mary back to the motel yesterday. Probably they'd just never seen an Arab or a man in a skirt before.

Sayyid Husayn turns back to the urinal, unzips his fly and pees.

Harvey is afraid to move. He can tell The Companion does not believe what he has said. Harvey can't figure out what he is expected to say. He decides to keep up his lie. Harvey swallows with difficulty and wonders what the fuck he'd hoped to accomplish by coming back here. He realizes he should urinate. He unbuckles his belt and unbuttons the fly of his Levis'. He is ready to piss when he realizes The Companion is staring down at his penis. Harvey blushes and a smile squirms across The Companion's lips. Now he can't relax enough to open his urinary tract at all.

Maybe this kid just wants a blowjob. Sayyid Husayn considers this a minute and then discards the idea.

Sayyid Husayn finishes, zips up his slacks and turns and walks the few feet to the mirrors over the two sinks. The kid still has not pissed. He watches the boy's back. His narrow waist and broad shoulders beneath his white T-shirt, his shoulder-length brown hair parted in the middle. Sayyid Husayn watches and combs his own short black hair.

Harvey manages a trickle and decides that is good enough. Harvey turns around as he fastens up his jeans and glances up into the mirror The Companion is in front of. The Companion is running a comb through His hair, and Harvey catches a metallic glint from inside The Companion's suit coat. Harvey stops and stares. With His hands at His head, elbows pointing out to either side, the revolver in its shoulder holster is plainly visible.

The Companion stops combing. From behind those sunglasses Harvey feels The Companion's unsettling gaze. Harvey could swear His eyes are on Harvey's crotch. Although Harvey is four or five inches taller and probably 50 pounds heavier than The Companion he blushes violently and starts sweating profusely. He quickly tucks in his T-shirt and finishes buttoning and belting his jeans.

Sayyid Husayn washes and then slowly dries his hands and walks out. Harvey is not sure but he thinks The Companion smiled as He left.

Harvey explains to the others that The Companion is aware of their attentions. He does not elaborate on what else happened in the bathroom. Sheila has already sent Fred and Raeann to follow The Companion to wherever The Lady is.

41

The sun finally sets around 10 o'clock and the temperature drops a little. Mary peeks out from behind motel room curtains. He sees that night has arrived and immediately his spirits rise. Now Mary is the one restless to go out.

Mary searches through his suitcase for something to wear. Sayyid Husayn performs his night prayer. This done he puts a cassette of PiL's "Second Edition" in the boombox Ruby and Murrow gave them to travel with. Then he starts with the little bit of shuffling and swaying that to him is dancing. As he dances Sayyid Husayn thinks about the kids in the cafe and decides not to tell Mary about them. It's not worth getting Mary all edgy over.

Mary settles on a short olive skirt and a sleeveless black T-shirt. He goes down the block to a liquor store and buys a pint of brandy because he finished off the rest of the gin while Sayyid Husayn was on his walk. By the time he gets back Sayyid Husayn is out of the shower and toweling dry. They work their way through half the pint and decide to go out for a stroll.

Even with the sun gone the air is still hot, dry and motionless. They walk and arrive in a neighborhood of industrial facilities. In an alley they climb a fire escape ladder three stories to the roof of this warehouse to see if there is any sort of breeze up there. There is a slight one. They settle down along the edge of the roof above the alley they'd just climbed up from.

Sayyid Husayn sits with his legs curled under and to one side. He leans on the raised brick rim of the roof. His body is turned facing Mary but most of his attention is on looking out at Spokane's lights and the alley below. Mary is resting with his lower back against the roof's two-foot-high brick edge. Legs crossed at the ankles, stretched out in front of him. The roof is flat and black, punctuated by several large metal vent hoods. The fire escape they came up has a twin directly opposite on the other side of the roof.

"Alright... so here we are, Spokane. Now what? The shopping was okay... but I don't see there being many employment opportunities here, for two guys like us... with our sorts of skills..."

Sayyid Husayn doesn't bother to reply. It's nice and hot here. But it's true, there's even less doing here than in Everett. He watches the lights of downtown Spokane twinkle and shimmer.

Not so far away a car screeches around a corner. Another corner and another. Each time they hear the tires squeal the car is closer to where they are perched. Closer and closer and it registers with both of them that a car is rapidly approaching bearing persons unknown. Sayyid Husayn sits up and leans out over the edge of the roof trying to see something of the approaching vehicle. One, then two more sharp loud turns and the car is just south of the building they're on.

Mary starts to get up and suddenly there are head-lights shooting down the alley jumping and jerking from pavement to walls as a large, late-model four-door sedan (maybe a Pontiac or Oldsmobile) plows through the alley over bumps and potholes.

Mary and Sayyid Husayn scuttle back away from the edge. They hear the car slam to a stop and doors fly open. Mary's heart is thudding violently. He wishes he'd brought more than just the six spare rounds he always keeps in his coin purse. Sayyid Husayn requests the blessings and presence of God, the Messenger Muhammad (pbuh) and the blessed Elder. Both men have their pistols drawn and the safeties off.

At the first rush of adrenaline Mary flashes that maybe the Fiances somehow know they are up here. Sayyid Husayn has similar thoughts as he wonders if he dismissed those kids being Fiances too quickly. But the loudness and recklessness of the approach and there being only one car makes them doubt it is some sort of ambush. Mary doubts that it's the police, but he keeps this possibility in mind.

Mary starts to move off in the direction of the fire escape ladder on the other side of the warehouse. Sayyid Husayn grabs Mary's lower arm and shakes his head no. He gestures to the edge of the roof they'd been leaning on. Mary shrugs and nods. Sayyid Husayn starts crawling on his belly, regardless of the suit he is wearing and Mary crouches on the balls of his feet, rubbing the grip of his revolver with his thumb and keeping an eye on the other ladder.

Sayyid Husayn slides the top half of his face over the brick lip so he can see below. Four men have a fifth, hands secured behind him, and are dragging him from the back of the sedan. They pull him in front of the car so that he is in the glare of the headlights. The four captors set about torturing the captive as he lies on the asphalt. Sayyid Husayn ducks back and scoots over to Mary. Despite the fact that nothing's been said out loud about it the first thing Sayyid Husayn whispers into his boyfriend's ear is:

"They're not here for us. They got this guy tied up on the ground. They're startin' to work him over. Check it out."

He moves rapidly back to the edge. Mary does not find the idea of watching some poor shit getting maimed and pulverized very thrilling. Sayyid Husayn is already back perched like an angel studying the peculiarities of human suffering.

Mary hesitates. If he crawls to the edge then his slacks will undoubtedly be ruined. And if he crawls properly his knees will end up too scraped to wear short skirts for a while. Is it really worth it? His boyfriend looks back at him right then and gestures with his head for Mary to join him. Mary sighs and nods slightly to show he'll be right there.

Mary has to squint to make out precise details. Now there are five men around the prisoner. Three of them hold him tight to the asphalt while a fourth is crouching next to him. The fifth man, in a light brown suit, is circling the prisoner and asking questions in a loud, but from the roof, indistinct voice. From the interrogator's actions and the prisoner's screaming responses Mary assumes the torturer is applying a knife, razor or some such thing. The harsh commanding voice punctuates between screams. The questioner walks around and around — a circling predator. The cutter makes a few moves with his right hand, the prisoner screams. The cutter looks up for further instructions. The man in the boss role stops and turns so that he is facing the building Mary and Sayyid Husayn are looking down from. He shouts something, his voice is a little clearer. At this angle his face is illuminated by the car headlights. Mary stares a little harder. Something is seeming more and more familiar about the inquisitor's voice and mannerisms. For just a second he reminds Mary of The Dictator. The torture victim's screams echo around the empty industrial neighborhood. Shrieks and loud frantic denials and pleading.

Sayyid Husayn touches Mary's arm and they both pull their heads back from the edge. Sayyid Husayn speaks with his lips right up to Mary's ear. His warm breath tickles the ear canal.

"Look, I wanna go down and get closer. There's something they want from that guy. Maybe it's something we can get first. If we can get close enough I think we could scare off those five guys without much problem."

Mary says nothing and nods his assent. His mind is still on the familiarity of the guy in the light brown suit. The more he lets that voice rattle around in his memory the closer to recognition he feels. Maybe up closer he'll remember.

They retreat to the ladder on the opposite side of the building. On the ground they quickly circle the warehouse to the alley they'd climbed up from. Smooth and careful they move up the alley, keeping to the walls. The screams and demands are getting clear and loud. Crouched 15 or so yards away behind a garbage dumpster Mary listens closely. That voice is so very familiar. Mary chews his lower lip and fiercely rubs the butt of his revolver with his right thumb. The man's identity is so close now. It's not The Dictator of course. But it is connected somehow with him. Someone at De Ville's. Not The Dictator, but at The Dictator's private booth. A lesser voice. Mary suddenly looks up and leans out so he can see the man. Sayyid Husayn pulls him back and scowls like what the fuck are you doing. Mary grabs Sayyid Husayn's coat sleeve and presses his lips to the other man's ear.

"That guy... the one that's asking all the questions, the guy walking around.... He hung around De Ville's..."

Sayyid Husayn scrutinizes his boyfriend.

"Yeah?"

"Yeah, I'm sure of it. Something seemed real familiar when we were up on the roof. His name is... uh... Covoe! Yeah, Bill Covoe. He was just working his way up to being seated at The Dictator's table when Burwell and I... started dating. I bet he's still Fiance. Maybe they set up a franchise in Spokane and Covoe got it."

Sayyid Husayn thinks about this and then nods slowly. He moves to the other side of Mary and studies the length of alley between them and the Fiances. He points to a loading dock up and across from them on the other side of the alley. Mary nods and Sayyid Husayn scurries over there. From that position Sayyid Husayn points to something farther ahead on Mary's side. By sliding over and looking through the space between the dumpster and the wall Mary can see that there is another dumpster parallel to Sayyid Husayn's position. The Fiances are too preoccupied with their prisoner to notice Mary duck momentarily into the alley and back out of sight behind a dumpster a few yards closer.

The victim's screams have faded to low guttural wails and moans. The torturer stands up, holding the bloody knife out away from his clothes and shrugs at his boss. The man Mary ID'd as Bill Covoe kicks the guy on the ground.

"Damnit!"

"I tried Mr. Covoe. If he knows anything about the stuff I don't have the tools here to get it out of him. Let's take'm back to the basement and I'll use electricity. Much more of this and he's not gonna be able to tell us anything, ever..."

"I told you nothing too deep. You're s'posed to be good at this stuff dumbshit!"

Covoe turns and repeatedly kicks the prisoner.

"Motherfucking pile of shit! Damnit! I want to go back and tell Hansen what he wants to know so he'll get the fuck outta my town. Go back to Seattle and leave me alone!

"If we go back now Hansen'll take over the job and have one of his Seattle boys do the work. And I'll be in shit with the bosses. Goddamnit! I'd just like to kill this asshole nice and slow."

Covoe slams his shoe into the man's crotch.

"Listen fuckface, start telling me things I wanna hear! In two minutes I'm gonna start using this guy's knife myself to cut your fuckin' dick off and force-feed it to ya! You hearing me asshole faggot!"

He draws his leg back to kick again. In his frenzy he has not seen Mary take a couple steps into the alley and crouch — legs bent at the knee, one in front and one behind and raise the .38. Covoe's men are too focused on their chief's anger to keep an eye on the alley they assume is empty.

The foot swings forward but never makes contact with flesh. Mary lightly squeezes the trigger and Covoe is knocked over, sideways. A hole just the right size for a rat to come and go punched through his neck by the hollow-point slug. The four other Fiances all turn. Sayyid Husayn takes a step forward and snaps off two shots before they can draw their weapons.

Eighty seconds max and three Fiances are down. One returns fire wildly, trying to cover his and another guy's retreat to their car. They crank it up, shove it into reverse and careen backward down the alley. Sayyid Husayn fires twice more, jabbing holes in the passenger side of the windshield. Once the car's out of the alley and racing away Mary and Sayyid Husayn move in on their catch. First to Covoe, then the other two Fiances. Checking that each one is indeed wearing the silver band of skulls they shoot them point-blank in the head for good measure. Wallets and pockets are rifled for any cash. Covoe is wearing a watch and jewelry that might be of some value but with nowhere to unload them Mary satisfies himself with smashing in the face of the watch and dropping the gold bracelet in a dumpster.

They finally return and kneel down next to the victim. His face is streaked with blood, a mess of small cuts of varying depths. His breathing is labored. His eyes are closed. Mary and Sayyid Husayn drag him to a wall and sit him up against it. Sayyid Husayn leans forward and cuts loose the man's bound wrists. Hands flop to his sides. Sayyid Husayn starts to stand up and at that instant the guy's eyes snap open and his bloody hands jerk out and clutch Sayyid Husayn's suit sleeves. Sayyid Husayn winces slightly at the blood on his clothes but says nothing, just looks the man in the eyes. The man sits there clutching the jacket and staring. Mary shakes his head like no-good too-late long-gone any-minute-now. He points his fingers like a gun at the man's head. He pulls an imaginary trigger. Sayyid Husayn shakes his head slightly no. Mary rolls his eyes. He figures the guy is a waste of time. Mary'd intervened just to spite the Fiances not to rescue this guy.

The man opens his mouth and spits out blood, he manages to talk.

"Please... please... help me... please, oh god..."

He spits a little more blood and takes short rasping breaths.

"... a doctor... please..."

He whines with pain and looks from one face to the other. Mary almost replies with a clever retort but holds himself to a brief sneer. He says in a cool offhand voice:

"Yeah, well, there's nothing we can do for you... we can't take you to a doctor or hospital... or call any cops..."

At the word "cops" the man tries to stand, there's a look of panic on his bloody face.

"No... no cops... please... shit no cops... you help me... I got, I got this stuff... they... but I... I didn't, I didn't tell... help me, and I'll... tell you where it... all is..."

This lengthy speech wears him out and he slumps against the wall. Sayyid Husayn and Mary simultaneously lean in closer. Suddenly both are afraid he will die too soon.

"*Stuff?!* Whaddaya got? Where is it?"

"I hid... it... buried it... I didn't tell... I didn't..."

"*Where?* Where is it? *What* is it!"

"Come on, help... me... I'll tell you... it's... far away... but I know exactly... where..."

His mouth slackens, his head slumps. Mary and Sayyid Husayn both reach for him.

"Shit, we gotta do something quick..."

Sayyid Husayn uses his already stained suit sleeve to wipe away blood that is trickling more and more steadily from the guy's mouth.

"Did you take it from them? The Fiances? A rip-off?"

The man's blood-smeared eyes flutter back open.

"I... they knew... somehow they knew... it was me... that got it..."

"Okay, okay. Shhh... lay back. We'll get you outta here."

"No way we can get him all the way back to the motel. Maybe we can stash him somewhere and go get our car."

Mary and Sayyid Husayn lift the man to his feet as gently as they can. But upright it is apparent that he's worse off than they thought. A couple of steps and his knees buckle. Mary and Sayyid Husayn exchange looks.

"Shit! I don't fucking see how they were gonna get him anywhere and have him still be alive when they got there. We gotta find out what he's talking about, and where the fuck it is."

They lower him back down against a wall.

"If there really is anything. He's bad off and he knows it. He'd say anything..."

The man has passed out. Mary remembers he's got the last half of the pint of brandy in his purse. It'll either wake the guy up or kill him. Mary gets it out and splashes it into the man's mouth. The man coughs and cries out in pain, blood and brandy splatter from his mouth. He wakes up grunting with pain. Mary starts talking to him in a kindly soothing voice.

"Okay honey. Just sit there. We got help coming for you. No no, not the cops. We got this — friendly doctor we know. He's on the way right now. Real sympathetic type. Know what I mean? So now, before he shows up, and things get... hectic again, you... you should tell us what it is you... buried. And where."

Mary's tone slips into urgency and insistence. The trickle of blood from the man's mouth has now become a steady stream; he coughs and looks from Mary to Sayyid Husayn; he smiles up at them. But the blood on his face prevents certainty about this. He squints trying to focus on Mary.

"You're cute babe... thanks... don't worry babe..."

He shifts his mostly unseeing gaze to Sayyid Husayn.

"Now... when you get it all... I want you to... buy this chick something... real nice... nice... it's all safe... nice... and safe in Kansas City... Kansas... City... it's still... I checked... in May... still... nice... and safe..."

"It's in Kansas City? What is it? Where in Kansas City? Where'd you get it from? What is it?"

"12th... Street... Vine... 12th... and Vine..."

He convulses sharply and whines and shivers. He looks in Mary's direction and then his head drops, chin to chest. Head lolls to one side.

"12th Street and Vine? Vine what? Avenue? Street? Place? What?! What?!"

"Nah. He's out again... we gotta go..."

Sayyid Husayn says this quiet and soft in case the man isn't totally unconscious.

"But if we leave him, and he... recovers... he might remember he told us about his stash and fly there or something before we even have a chance to look for it. I think, we should, you know..."

They stand up. Sayyid Husayn keeps looking at the man on the ground sort of hoping signs of life will stir in him and he'll say something else a little more precise about what and where. But no.

"Come on Husayn. We gotta go! Those two fucks could

be on their way back with reinforcements."

Sayyid Husayn crouches again and uses two fingers to search the guy's neck for a pulse. Finding only a feeble erratic one he stands up, pursing his lips.

"Well, we can't just leave'm. If the Fiances get him alive he might end up spilling what he told us, and more, to them... and like you said, if he lives and gets away somehow he's gonna know we didn't do nothing for him and that we know he buried something valuable in Kansas City at 12th and Vine..."

Mary raises an eyebrow and gives his boyfriend a look. Slowly and quietly he takes his revolver back out of his purse and gently puts it against the man's head.

"Goodbye, and thanks sweetie..."

Mary pulls the trigger, smashing away most of the top and back of the man's skull. He puts his revolver away and gives Sayyid Husayn another look.

They take off running in the direction opposite from where the car had come and gone. Multiple blocks later Mary and Sayyid Husayn are in the edge of the down-town area. They pause to catch their breath. Their smokers' lungs burning and heaving from the exertion. Sayyid Husayn empties the suit coat's pockets and stuffs the coat in a trashcan. He uses a white cotton handker-chief with some spit to try to get some of the guy's blood splatters off his shirt front. Failing, he takes off the shirt and wads it up and tosses it in with the suit coat. He checks to see that his A-shirt is unstained. His wind somewhat returned, he asks:

"Where... is... Kansas City..."

"I think... it's... it's in, Kansas... or maybe... Missouri... I dunno..."

42

In their motel room Sayyid Husayn is on the bed studying their road atlas. Mary is soaking his slacks in cold water in the bathroom sink seeing if he can get some of the bloodstains out. Sayyid Husayn slams the atlas closed.

"You weren't shitting me. There are two fucking Kansas Citys. At least they're right next to each other. But I can't find no fucking 12th or Vine! The fucking city maps in this thing are too small to have enough detail!"

Mary wrings out the slacks and drapes them over the shower curtain rod. He goes over to the bed and flops down next to Sayyid Husayn.

"Whatever. We'll just have to go to both of them won't we. We can get better city maps when we get there."

"And he did say 12th and Vine, right?"

"Yeah, yeah. 12th and Vine. You heard him as well as I did."

"Alright, alright. He also said he buried it. And that he checked on it just a couple months ago. So it must be pretty easy to get at, right? Not under some parkinglot or building or something. That's something at least."

Sayyid Husayn still looks a little worried. Mary picks

up the atlas and sets it on the small side table. He pulls
Sayyid Husayn closer.

"Are you all packed?"

"Sure, sure."

Sayyid Husayn watches TV but still worries. He can
clearly see that this is a test, a trial of faith. God willing
they will solve the puzzle and their just rewards will be
at hand. Mary is thinking about Edith, and he's disappointed that killing those Fiances did nothing to allevi-
ate his guilt or sense of failure. He clenches and
unclenches his jaw. Thinking about the dead Fiances
leads Mary to wondering where they had Edith buried.
He sighs and swings his feet off the bed.

"I'm gonna write another postcard to mom and grama."

Mary listens to the music and mulls Sayyid Husayn over
and over in his mind. Sayyid Husayn is already asleep.
Mary has turned off the volume of the TV and is playing
a cassette of Nico.

His brain stirs and sifts through a not particularly
linear shuffle of perspectives and hunches. Randomly
divided into segments or episodes by a recurring snapshot
from several years ago. Mary in a cheap red cotton
summer-type dress. No sleeves, low-cut neck. He's
holding his favorite revolver at waist level, pointing it
at the camera. Mary is standing very close to Sayyid
Husayn. Sayyid Husayn is in his shirt sleeves. He has his
left arm around Mary's waist and his other hand is in a
trouser pocket. Both are wearing dark sunglasses, both

are smiling. The scenery behind them is indistinguish-
able concrete and sunlight.

Always conservative in his personal movements Mary
allows only minor tremors and twitches to express the
shivers of memory along his psyche. A tumble of image
and inference. Years and years, segueing from here and
gone. Emotions come and go in washes of sweat.
Trailing off in whirling shadows. Shifting in the light of
conscious consideration... hindsight... rewind replay cut
from particular to particular of the last time they
fucked... something specific from the most recent time...
another of The Ninety-Nine Names of The Divine on his
lips.

Sayyid Husayn's emaciated sharp angles, curled up
beside him, emanating heat.

43

Sayyid Husayn is standing leaning his butt against the
car door. He drops the last of a cigarette and taps it out
with the toe of his left shoe (a black wing tip).

Inside the car the stereo pauses and then an even
slower Lebanese poptune by Mona Geagea comes on.
Sayyid Husayn resumes rhythmically swaying his head
from side to side. Lips silently synching along. He turns
around, leans in the open window on the passenger side
and ups the volume. Mon Geagea's crooning drone
becomes a thunderous wail.

The couple from the motel room next to Sayyid Husayn and Mary's are also loading their car for the start of the day's travels. These two cars are separated by two empty parking spaces. When Sayyid Husayn cranks the music the man stops packing in suitcases and stands up. He stares over the roof of his Subaru at the back of Sayyid Husayn's head. His wife notices her husband's glaring and joins him in it. The husband says something rude. Probably something racist and/or homophobic. The music is too loud to hear him. But the man and the woman's scowls convey scorn and distaste.

The morning is very bright and already hot. The motel room's doorway is a black rectangle in the white walls. Mary pushes open the screen door as he pulls the inner door almost all the way shut.

Seeing Mary come out Sayyid Husayn moves around the front of the car to the driver's side. His right hand touching Mary's stomach as they pass. He adjusts the front seat forward so he can reach the pedals. Mary opens the passenger door. Bracing his right knee on the front seat he leans into the back, searching through their stuff piled on the rear seat. Just making sure some particular item has not been left in the room. Satisfied everything is there Mary goes back and pulls the inner motel room door firmly closed.

Mary lets go of the screen door and it bangs shut. Mary pauses on the sidewalk and smiles at Sayyid Husayn as he lights a Lucky Strike. He sees the couple by the car two spaces away staring at him. His very dark sunglasses prevent them immediately realizing their rude behavior has been spotted. Mary stands there drawing on his Lucky Strike and exhaling though his nose. Slowly he turns his head in their direction so that it is obvious he is staring back. Aware their challenge has been met they quickly drop their gazes and retreat into the Subaru. As they back out Mary tosses his cigarette at them. The smoldering Lucky Strike lands on the Subaru's windshield and rolls off the hood.

Once he's seated and the door is closed Mary raises his ass up enough to run his hands underneath and smooth his skirt. He leans forward and adjusts the stereo volume down a bit. Sayyid Husayn starts the engine. He snubs out his cigarette before pulling out. He steers to the lot's exit and waits for Mary to start navigating. Mary is studying the road atlas.

"Montana. Bozeman by tonight. That's, uh, not quite 400 miles. We can do that easy."

He looks up and smiles. Sayyid Husayn is still waiting for directions. Mary catches on.

"Oh. Uh, left. I-90 east is what we want. Keep an eye out for signs."

Sayyid Husayn maneuvers into traffic headed east out of Spokane. He reaches into the breast pocket of his shirt and finds his cigarette pack empty.

"I got another pack in the glove box. Light me one will you?"

Sayyid Husayn reaches his right hand over to Mary's thigh. He reaches down a few inches below the hem and slides the fabric up to expose more of his boyfriend's leg, he leaves his hand there. The dashboard lighter pops out ready. Sayyid Husayn removes his hand to accept the lit cigarette. He puffs once on it and says:

"Montana... how many days from there to the Kansas Citys do you think?"

"Two or three. There! Get over a lane. The sign says I-90 right lane."

Sayyid Husayn accelerates up the on-ramp and Mary leans over the seat to roll down the back windows. The roar of hot air and Mona Geagea grind and pulse together. Mary taps his foot to the central rhythm of the music.

44

Mary's singing along with the Sonic Youth cassette which has replaced Mona Geagea. Sayyid Husayn is humming along reveling in the hot weather. Mary takes out his reserve .38, unloads, dismantles and starts in cleaning it.

Mary's neck is getting stiff looking down inspecting the chambers as he pulls the bit of rag through each one. He stops, sets the revolver parts and rag to his left on the seat. He rolls his neck and shoulders to stretch the muscles. Sitting back Mary looks ahead at the low, rolling brown hills. His eyes lock onto six figures standing on a hilltop alongside the highway maybe 80, 100 yards up the road. Strange.

Mary doesn't take his eyes off them as he feels around in the glove box for his other revolver, which is loaded. At 70 miles an hour they are in view, alongside and passed before he gets a good look at them. But even with the car jetting by Mary can see they are waving their arms at him and propped in front of them is a large piece of white cardboard (4' x 6') with big, hand-painted lettering on it that reads:

"HAIL MARY!"

Those two words are quite legible. The six sets of eyes are on Mary.

"Husayn! Stop!"

Turning around on the seat Mary scrambles to his knees and leans out the window, peering back at the kids on the hill. The kids see the car has stopped and they turn the sign toward the car. They are excitedly jumping around and gesturing even more frantically. Mary is sure these people he does not know are waving at him.

Sayyid Husayn was wrapped up in thoughts about the treasure they are going to find so he has seen nothing. Once the car is stopped he is looking around and reaching under his suit coat neatly folded next to him on the front seat for his own revolver. But all he sees is this small group of kids on a hill a couple of dozen yards back. Sure they're waving their arms around and the sign says "HAIL MARY!" but they don't look like any sort of threat. From this distance he cannot recognize them as the kids from the cafe. He wonders if Mary knows these people.

Mary isn't saying anything. Just leaning out of the car

window with his left hand's palm propping him up on
the door and looking back at them. The cassette is
playing loud enough to easily drown out whatever the
distance might have allowed Sayyid Husayn and Mary
to hear otherwise. Mary still doesn't say anything, just
keeps rubbing the grip of his revolver with the thumb of
his right hand. Sayyid Husayn decides maybe he should
go back toward the hill and get a better look. He
accelerates the car in reverse. Mary jerks his head back
inside the car and shouts:

"No! No just keep driving. Get us outta here..."

Sayyid Husayn's foot pounces on the brake and he
purses his lips in mild irritation. He snubs out his Raleigh
in the dashboard ashtray, shifts into drive and stomps
down on the gas pedal. The car screeches forward and
Mary is thrown back against the seat. This sudden
motion causes Mary's right hand to tense up and his
finger to pull the trigger — but of course the safety is on.
Mary rights himself quickly enough to see the six
strangers disappear into the horizon. With his left hand
he tries to keep his hair from blowing in his eyes.

Mary sits down again but says nothing. Firmly gripping the revolver now lying in his lap. His skirt is a
mustard yellow, the vinyl car seat is gray and the Smith
& Wesson is matte black. He leans forward and pushes
in the dashboard lighter.

Sayyid Husayn looks over at Mary a couple of times,
he keeps his foot down on the gas. Mary shakes his head.

"Okay... you can lay off the speed now."

Sayyid Husayn eases off the gas. He puzzles on the

incident a minute and then reaches up and turns Sonic
Youth down a bit. A slight jerk of his head up and back
points to the highway receding behind them as he says:

"I thought maybe you knew them... I mean the sign
and all..."

Mary grabs the lighter as soon as it pops out and
ignites another Lucky Strike. He shakes his head no. No.

"Fucking strange huh? No, I have no fucking idea
what that was all about. A buncha kids on a hill, like they
were waiting there, for us to go by."

"Pretty fucking weird. I mean that sign and all."

Mary shrugs and raises his eyebrows and twists his
lips.

"I dunno."

Mary shakes his head from side to side. Slides down
farther in the seat and exhales a cloud of smoke loudly.

"Whatever."

Mary's thumb still (but less frantically) massaging the
tiny crisscross of the textured plastic revolver butt.

45

The car disappears into the shimmering horizon. Sheila
silently mouths a last Hail Mary, tears are running from
her eyes. The others are all looking east. Except for the
wind there is silence. In a few minutes the intoxicating
glaze of Manifestation leaves Sheila's eyes and she looks
from friend to friend smiling and nodding. The six are

very pleased with themselves and the fact that the car actually stopped for them. The car stopped, the Queen of Angels leaned out the window and looked right at them. The look. An entire frame of reference and entire statement of blessing in Her face, the wind whipping the hair, the bold stare.

Sheila picks up one end of the sign and Harvey the other. The rest fall in behind them. Everyone heads for Harvey's car which is parked a quarter mile south along an access road.

Sheila stops, turns and glances east up I-90. She starts off again (kicking the tall grasses with each foot) but she halts after two paces. She looks back, her eyes following I-90 to the point on the horizon, shimmering and vague, where the Interstate disappears. Now there is only that slender black point of freeway to indicate the general direction The Lady has gone. Sheila takes a long and deep breath. Exhale.

A creeping smile (jagged and verging on dangerous) pulls along her lips. Genuflect and genuflect again. Sheila drops her end of the sign and takes off running for the car. The others dash pell-mell after her. Hooting and hollering, grabbing handfuls of the taller weeds and tossing them in the air.

The sign, function fulfilled, is left lying in the grass.

GOD & PLASTIC SURGERY
MARX, NIETZSCHE, FREUD AND THE OBVIOUS
JEREMY BARRIS

An unusual and intensive examination of the work
of the intellectual progenitors of contemporary
Western thought, with a battery of insights into
how to and how *not* to think, act, feel, eat, dress,
dance, take tea, or make love. Something like
equal parts Gertrude Stein and Wittgenstein,
this text is written with an eye on the concept of
justice, intended to provoke, upset, and
transfigure perceptions of modern culture.
Now Available — $12 postpaid

ON AN(ARCHY) AND SCHIZOANALYSIS
ROLANDO PEREZ

Using the "anti-oedipal" insights of Gilles Deleuze
and Félix Guattari's classic work on capitalism and
schizophrenia, Perez argues for "anti-fascist
strategies in everyday life," and reads Nietzsche,
literature, films and popular culture to critique
deep political sympathies and antagonisms. Treats
writers from Kafka to D. M. Thomas, filmmakers
like David Lynch, punk music and feminist theory.
Now Available — $10 postpaid